JESSICA MOORE

Murder At Ash Castle

A Susie Carter Mystery

Jessica Moore

Published by Next Page Press.

Next Page
Press

First published in Australia in 2016 by Moore Fiction.
Revised Edition published February 2018 by Next Page Press.

Copyright © 2018 Next Page Press

DEDICATION

Dedicated to Mrs. Oat.
Thanks for introducing me to the wonders of Cornwall.

FREE MYSTERY BOOKS

Love a good Murder Mystery?

If so join our newsletter list and receive free murder mystery books and updates from Next Page Press including new release news.

www.NextPagePress.com

JESSICA MOORE

1

SUSIE CARTER GASPED WITH SURPRISE. She did not believe what she had read, yet there it was in black and white. The letter had been delivered earlier by old Bill, but she didn't have time to open. Now she stood in her quaint living room somewhat in shock with the news.

'Oh goodness, Max, can you see what this means?'

Max wagged his tail in that way only Labradors can manage. He smiled at her and followed her up the hallway to the small table where her phone was located. Max had been her faithful companion for the last five years. Now he thought they were heading out for another walk.

'I must ring Margery and discuss the matter with her first.' Susie informed Max.

Nervously she fumbled through her address book until she found Margery's number. A lifelong friend, Margery had grown up with Susie in the small town of Middle Thorpe on the outskirts of York.

The phone barely rang before Margery picked it up. They both loved a good gossip, and usually, it was about small-town matters. Today was going to be different though, and Margery had sensed it in the air before the phone had a chance to ring more than once.

'Hello Margery dear, it's Susie.'

'Hello dear, how are you, and more importantly, what's new?' Margery inquired.

Unsure how to share the news with her closest friend Susie decided it was best to take a seat first. Max took a seat as well knowing he was going to have to be patient before he got his walk.

'Well, I'm not entirely sure how to tell you this.' Susie stated, a little breathless.

'Now take a deep breath dear and start at the beginning.' Margery calmed her, eager to hear the news, but not wanting to rush her.

'Well, the truth is I'm not sure what to make of this news.'

And that was the truth. The news that had just arrived by post was going to change everything. It was going to turn hers and Max's life upside down.

Margery was rightly intrigued. 'Well, what on earth is it?'

'A letter arrived this morning.' Susie continued.

'And?' Margery was more than curious, and growing frustrated with her friend.

'Well, do you remember my great Uncle Charles Ash III?' Susie asked. 'We visited him for summer holidays back when we were both a little sprightlier?'

'Yes of course.' She remembered him as being a slightly eccentric chap with a patch over his eye.

'Oh, you have a good memory.' Susie replied.

'Well that was some time ago, but I vaguely remember him.' Margery assured her, already concluding he must have passed on.

'Well, a letter came this morning from his solicitor. It seems he has passed on at the age of 92.' Susie said, a tear forming in the corner of her eye. She reached out for a tissue. Max gave her a reassuring nuzzle on the side of her leg.

'Oh, I am sorry dear. If I remember correctly, he was your last surviving relative, was he not?' Margery asked, her voice filled with concern. At least a trip down to Cornwall might be in order, for the funeral she thought to herself, already deciding what to pack.

'Yes, he was sadly.' Susie reflected on the fact that over the years her family had thinned out until now it was just her and Max.

'Well, I guess we will have to plan to attend the funeral.' Margery suggested. 'When is it scheduled for?'

Susie sighed with disbelief. 'They have already had it, apparently.'

On the one hand, she was glad not to have to attend another

wretched funeral. At 53 she had attended more than her fair share. On the other hand, a trip to Cornwall with Margery would have been a nice break.

'Oh, that's a bother.' Margery said, mentally unpacking her suitcase.

'But Margery, there is more news in the letter.' Susie said hesitantly. She wondered how she might inform her friend of the news. How would she take it?

'Well, what is it dear?'

'Well, it seems that as I am the only surviving relative of Charles that I am to inherit his property.' Susie explained.

'You don't say?' Margery said with delight. 'Do you mean?'

'Yes exactly!' Susie squealed. Max jumped to his feet and gave a little bark of delight. He may not know what they were talking about, but he sensed the excitement in the air and wanted to be part of it.

'Ash Castle?' Margery asked seeking confirmation.

'Yes!' Susie agreed. 'I am now the proud owner of a rundown old castle in Cornwall.'

'Oh! Good heavens. I am going to have to start calling you Lady Susan Carter from now on.' Margery roared with laughter. They both had a good old laugh and continued chatting about the contents of the letter.

'So, have you had a chance to consider what you might do with the old castle?' Margery asked considering all the possibilities.

'Well, I dare say I will sell it and invest the proceeds. Maybe we could take a little trip to the mainland in the summer if you like?' Susie suggested. Susie was generous with her close friends. She was fortunate enough to own her small, yet charming cottage, and lived a good life, so she liked to help where she could.

'That sounds delightful. From memory, the old castle needed some repair all those years ago when we visited.' Margery recalled. 'Do you know what state it's in these days at all?'

'I have no idea I'm afraid. The letter from the solicitors has asked me to come to Polmerton to meet with them next week.'

'Oh, how exciting for you.' Margery sighed with envy.

'There is one other thing Margery, and I'm not sure what to make of it.' Susie confided as the tone of her voice dropped from jubilant to melancholy.

Delighted by this most intriguing phone call Margery asked, 'What on earth is it?' She sensed the mood change of her friend and felt some concern.

'Well, the letter from the solicitors mentioned there is some mystery surrounding the circumstances of my uncle's death. It seems the police are making some inquiries.'

'You shouldn't be bothered with that dear. It's probably routine. He was, after all, old enough for one's time to be up.' Margery reassured her.

'You're quite right! I shouldn't fuss.' Susie said picking up her spirits.

'Yes, I mean it's not as though he was murdered now is it?' Margery said with a sinking feeling. It was a case of no filter between her thoughts and her mouth. The words were out there before she realized, and try as she might, there was no taking them back.

'Goodness, I hope not. There was no mention of wrongdoing as such.' Susie said.
Her mind went into overdrive.
She assured herself that nothing so exciting could ever possibly happen in a sleepy hollow like Polmerton. Margery enthusiastically agreed.

After chatting on for another ten or so minutes, mostly about where they might go on vacation once Ash Castle was sold, they said their goodbyes and hung up the phone.

Max who was used to waiting patiently while Susie was on the phone pulled his old body to his feet and gave a sharp bark towards the stand where his lead hung. He looked up at Susie with his adorable brown eyes and smiled.

'A jolly good idea,' she said patting him on the head as she reached for the lead. 'A brisk walk through the woods is just what we both need to clear our heads of all this excitement.'

2

One week later and Susie found herself seated in the boardroom of Sampson, Smith & Arlington law firm. She sat on one side of the mahogany desk waiting for Harold Sampson to enter the room.

She had traveled down from York to Polmerton in Cornwall with Max the day before. Polmerton, as it turned out, was a delightful fishing village nestled into a quiet part of the Cornish coast. It was probably not one of the most popular towns in Cornwall such as your St Ives or Penzance. This was a sleepy little village with a quaint atmosphere mostly untouched by the buzz of noisy tourists.

Susie glanced around the boardroom and marveled at the extensive collection of artwork on the walls, and the array of antique furnishings. She concluded that not much had changed at Sampson, Smith, and Arlington in the last decade or two.

Harold Sampson finally made his way into the boardroom and sat opposite Susie after introducing himself. He looked like he might be closing in on ninety years of age. His weak legs barely able to mobilize his equally frail frame.

Yet despite his fragile nature, he carried in a rather large folder and plonked it on the table in front of Susie. Dust scattered around the room vacating the spot now occupied by the file.

'Susan Carter, I assume?' Harold inquired peering down his long bony nose and over the top of his reading glasses. His yellow cardigan had a musty odor about it.

'Yes, that is correct Mr. Sampson,' she confirmed admiring his multi-colored floral bow tie. How is it that only eccentric lawyers could pull off the bow tie look these days? She wondered.

'Thank you for coming at such short notice,' he said as he opened the file on top and flicked through its contents. 'Your great Uncle Charles Ash III was a dear friend of mine. Known him since I was a boy you know.'

'You don't say? I had no idea,' Susie was intrigued. She had grown up not really knowing her great uncle. She had met him a few times, visiting once as a teenager with Margery, but for most of her life, he remained somewhat of a mystery to her. Perhaps in time, Mr. Sampson might be able to fill in some questions she had about her uncle.

'How well did you know Charles? If you don't mind my asking,' Sampson asked.

'Not that well really. In fact, I was hoping you might be able to fill in some gaps for me at some stage?'

Harold Sampson nodded in agreement.

Finally, he settled upon the document he had been looking for. He placed his glasses back in position ready to read the final will and testimony of Mr. Charles Ash III.

'Well I should warn you,' Sampson said clearing his throat. 'Charles was somewhat eccentric and grew increasingly so as the years progressed. He may have left everything to you, but it does come with some conditions which we need to discuss.'

Susie wondered what on earth he meant by warning her? Was the will not straightforward? Had he not left her Ash Castle after all? And what about these conditions? Her heart rate quickened as a million thoughts raced through her mind.

'The last will and testimony of Mr. Charles Ash III read this day in the presence of myself Harold Sampson lawyer for the deceased, and Ms. Susan Carter of Middle Thorpe, York' Sampson said launching into the document.

Susie literally held her breath as Sampson continued his appointed duty on behalf of his client.

A good thirty minutes later Susie found Max where he was seated in the foyer of Sampson, Smith & Arlington. He was glad to see her. Getting a pat around this smelly old place was proving more challenging than he was up for.

Susie gave Max a scratch behind the ears before undoing his lead. She thanked Chelse, the receptionist, for looking after Max and stepped out onto High Street in Polmerton.

Glancing around the small village she was taken by its quaint untouched nature. It was literally like stepping back in time to when Polmerton would have been a busy fishing village keeping all the locals supplied with fresh fish. The hills around Polmerton no doubt would have been littered with tin mines at various stages.

Susie sucked in a deep lung full of fresh salty sea air as a rather large seagull hovered overhead. She watched as a small fishing vessel headed out of the safe harbor and towards the open ocean on its next voyage.

She watched them depart the headlands and marveled at how her current situation was so similar. Should she leave the relatively safe harbor of the life she had always known in York and risk it all by taking on Ash Castle? Running a castle was not precisely what she trained for back in her college days.

'Well, Max, let's look at what may be our new home,' she said, and together they walked towards the car park to locate her trusty Land Rover.

Ash Castle may well be her new home, but as she had just discovered in her meeting with Harold Sampson, it came with some conditions attached.

Ash Castle sat on the outskirts of Polmerton about 7 miles away. It was a grand old castle standing high on a hill with panoramic views of the ocean and over the village of Polmerton.

Built in the 1400's to stop the French invading it had been extensively renovated on numerous occasions in the following six hundred or so years. The most recent significant renovation by Charles Ash himself, but that was a good thirty years ago now. The castle had been in the Ash family for six generations.

As she navigated the Land Rover around the windy road with lovely woody trees to either side leading to the castle boundary and gates, she pondered the conditions imposed on her as the new owner.

She finally arrived at the gates and braked as several plump wooly sheep grazed on the long grass growing up the middle of the road.

'Oh, look Max what a lovely sight,' she said looking up the driveway to the grand castle. From the entry gates, you looked up the hill where Ash Castle sat dominating the landscape.

Max jumped on the passenger seat to get a better view. He gave a bark or two in agreement with her. It did look rather grand. His tail thumping against the leather seats and Susie's arm. He was going to enjoy exploring the grounds and woodlands surrounding the castle.

Susie pointed the Land Rover up the driveway, and a few moments later they arrived in the car park in front of the castle entry.

In days gone by, the castle would have been home to an entire village of people. It was vast with walls wrapping around the hill. In modern times renovations had been confined to just the west wing which offered the best views across the bay and Polmerton.

Helping Max out of the car Susie found herself more than just a little nervous. She straightened her skirt and walked up the stone steps to the double oak doors with giant brass knockers.

'Well, here goes,' she said looking down at Max. He had taken a seat and returned her glance with his tongue hanging out of the side of his mouth. His enlarged brown eyes giving her an encouraging look.

Reaching up to knock on the door, Susie got the shock of her life as it swung open before her knuckles reached the timber. Standing before her was an elderly gentleman in what looked like his seventies or eighties. He stood in full butler uniform with polished black shoes and white satin gloves.

'Oh, hello there,' Susie said somewhat nervously.

'Welcome Ma'am' Woolsworth the Butler said rather officially. He swung the door open to allow her entry.

'Why thank you. I am ...'

'Yes Ma'am. You are Lady Susan Carter,' he stated matter-of-fact and offered her a gloved hand to shake.

Susie shook his hand while encouraging him to call her Susie.

'And you are?' she asked.

'Woolsworth Ma'am. Butler Woolsworth' he replied as he helped Susie with her coat. 'I've been the butler here at Ash Castle for a good fifty years or more. So, if there is anything you need to know, then do not hesitate to ask.'

Max shot past Woolsworth and started sniffing around the entry foyer. In the corner next to the massive oak stairwell stood a Knights Armor. Max took an immediate interest in it and sniffed every inch of the Armor.

Somewhat horrified at the site of the dog in the residence, Woolsworth let out a cry of disapproval. He went to grab Max by the collar, but Max darted to one side almost knocking over an exotic looking vase. Woolsworth sucked in a deep breath with a horrified look on his face.

'Ma'am would you like me to put the beast out in the kennels?' he said, trying to predict Max's next move.

'Oh! Good heavens no! Max come here.' Susie responded with disbelief. 'Max is an indoor dog Woolsworth.' Max sat by her side thumping his tail with joy.

'I feared as much,' the butler responded tersely. With that, Woolsworth walked down a side hallway sighing to himself. He was muttering under his breath as he disappeared around the corner.

'Well Max, I guess it's just you and me,' she laughed to herself unsure what to do next.

'Hello, there,' a welcoming voice came down the stairs startling both Susie and Max. They both looked up in unison to see a shapely pair of young legs coming down the steps.

Megan Lane was twenty-seven years of age and walked with the confidence that comes with youth. She came down the stairs in a flash and presented herself to Susie and Max.

'You must be Lady Susan Carter,' she declared offering her delicate hand to Susie to shake.

'Why yes, indeed I am.' Susie said, shaking her hand. 'And who might you be sweetie?'

'I am Megan Lane, your personal assistant. But you can call me Meg. Everyone does.' She informed Susie, beaming from ear to ear. Meg was so happy that someone as lovely as Susan Carter had come to run Ash Castle. It would be a change from the last five horrid years of working for the old man Ash she thought.

'And who is this adorable fellow?' Meg asked with delight as she got down on her knees to greet Max. Max was delirious with happiness as he received some of the best pat's he had had all day.

His tail worked overtime as the two of them fell instantly in love with each other.

'This is Max. Max meet Megan Lane,' Susie said doing the introductions.

Max barked a welcome to Meg.

'Now Lady Carter, let me first give you a tour of your new home and then we can get you settled in.' Meg said taking control of the situation.

'Oh, please dear call me Susie.'

'Susie, it is then, but I insist you call me Meg.' Meg shot them both a smile before leading them on a tour of the ground floor.

Meg showed Susie to her room which was, of course, the master bedroom of the castle. It was impressive and grand. Susie joked with Max that the bedroom alone was bigger than their cottage back home.

Meg went to find Woolsworth and instruct him to bring up the luggage from the Land Rover. Susie opened the double doors leading onto the balcony. It was higher than expected and a gentle sea breeze swept across her. She leaned against the balcony, and from here the views were simply breathtaking.

After settling in, Susie met Meg in the office. The office was a shared space with a large grand desk which was formerly Charles Ash's, and a somewhat smaller desk for Meg.

It occurred to Susie that Meg was the one who did all the work in the office.

In fact, Susie was not really planning on spending a lot of time in the office at all if she could avoid it. Her thoughts had already turned to the garden and getting that into shape. She imagined the stunning rose garden she and Max could cultivate over time.

'Right, I know you have a lot you wish to discuss with me young Meg, however, the first order of business that we must sort out is the desk.' Susie said taking control.

'Whatever do you mean?' Meg became concerned. 'Is my desk too messy for you?'

'Not at all, dear no.' Susie laughed at Meg's concern. 'On the contrary, as you will be spending more time here than me the first thing we need to do is swap desks. You should have the larger one.'

The next fifteen minutes were spent swapping over desks.

Meg sat back in the old leather swivel chair and felt delighted to have such a magnificent desk to work from. She was going to love working for Lady Susan Carter.

'Now Meg, I know you have a lot you need to discuss with me, so over to you.'

'Okay, well where to start really.' Meg said and shuffled three piles of paper around. 'There are a few things we need to consider such as bills, then, of course, there is upkeep and maintenance of the castle itself, and there are wages.' Meg was becoming a little flustered at the thought of the mounting bills and operating costs of the castle.

The truth was the castle cost a small fortune to maintain and run each year. It needed constant maintenance and renovation. Then there was the cost just to run it on a day-to-day basis. And of course, there were wages for Meg and Woolsworth, not to mention the groundskeepers and a sundry list of others who all did their bit to keep Ash Castle running.

Forty minutes later after going through everything with Meg, Susie sighed with despair.

'So, let me get this clear Meg dear.' Susie said wanting to get absolute clarity on the current situation. 'You are saying that currently, we owe approximately 231,000 pounds for maintenance works either carried out or needing to be carried out?'

'Yes, that is correct.' Meg agreed, beginning to feel a little guilty.

'And the annual running costs including wages and the like is 110,000 pounds?' Susie asked not able to believe it would cost so much to run an old castle.

'Well yes, that is correct,' Meg agreed

'Oh dear,' Susie exclaimed resting her head in her hand for a moment. 'And how much money is in the accounts now then?'

'Currently, there are about 37,000 pounds across a number of accounts,' Meg informed her.

'Oh dear, this is worse than I thought.' Susie said with concern, 'Does Ash Castle generate any revenue?'

Meg was expecting the question. 'No not today. Five years ago, it did raise money through visitor days. The tourists would pay money to come and poke around. But that all ended when Mr. Ash became ill.'

'So there has been no income in five years?'

'That's right. We had a healthy bank account back then, but it has since been used up.' Meg said feeling somewhat stressed by the situation.

Susie sat back in her chair with her arm hanging over the side stroking Max. She felt overwhelmed by this new information. On the one hand, it seemed a jolly good thing to inherit a castle. But on the other, she now felt trapped by the windfall.

In the meeting with Harold Sampson, she had been informed that while she had indeed inherited the castle, the conditions attached to it were two-fold. Firstly, that she could not sell the castle as it was to remain either in the family or gifted back to the National Trust, and secondly, that the hired help, namely Woolsworth and Megan Lane where to be kept on in employment as they were both long-time family friends of the Ash's. Both the Woolsworth's, and the Lanes had worked at Ash Castle since the time when the first Ash moved in.

'Thanks for the update Meg,' Susie said regaining her composure. 'I think what we both need are a good stiff drink and an early night. These challenges are always best faced at the dawn of a new day with fresh heads.'

3

Susie arose the next morning as she always did. A wet nose nudging her hand signaling that the sleeping was done, and it was time to get up. Max wagged his tail eagerly from side to side excited as always to see her.

'Morning, my dear boy,' she said patting the side of the bed. Max needed no further encouragement, and with his two front paws on the side of the bed, nuzzled his head into her chest. There were few delights he enjoyed more than a morning scratch on the back of the head. Except for walks. And treats.

Marveling at how refreshed she felt, Susie informed Max that it might well have been one of the best night's sleep she'd had in longer than she could remember.

After the usual routine of showering and dressing, she wondered downstairs where Woolsworth had made a morning cup of tea. Earl Grey no less, accompanied with a hard-boiled egg and sourdough toast buttered just the way she liked it.

'Woolsworth, how on earth did you know what I have for breakfast?' she inquired gratefully but fascinated he would know such details.

'Thirty-seven years ago, Ma'am, you visited Ash Castle for a week. That is what you requested each morning. I figured old habits die hard. I trust it's to your satisfaction?'

'Remarkable.' Susie exclaimed barely able to remember what happened yesterday. Let alone thirty-something years ago. 'That's a real talent you have,' she said as she slurped at the yoke.

Woolsworth, thinking that four-legged animals belonged in the yard, went to take Max by the collar and haul him outside. Max was having none of it and growled entirely out of character.

'Max!' Susie cried out. He had never growled at anyone before she thought.

Woolsworth wandered off a little startled. Susie heard him, over the chomping of toast, muttering about beasts belonging in the yard, not in the kitchen.

Paperwork was piled in an office in-tray next to the small breakfast table. She reached for it deciding she would rummage through it while she drank her Earl Grey.

Nothing of significance was found. The usual collection of utility bills, letters to old friends, travel brochures, and requests for money from various charities. She almost gave up on finding anything vaguely interesting when she came across a typed letter addressed to Mr. Charles Ash III.

The letter was very formal and was from a Douglas Hamilton. It appeared Mr. Hamilton, a local Realtor, had become a touch disgruntled over a recent property deal. The details, however, seemed to be patchy, so she tossed it back on the pile to sort through with Meg later.

Finishing up her tea, the silence of the still morning air was broken by an overly excited Meg thundering down the stairs. She was shrieking like death itself was following her.

'Good heavens Meg. Are you okay?' Susie yelled leaping to her feet. Max may have been aging, but when excitement was in the air, he was quick to leap on all fours alongside his master.

'Oh my!' Meg was clearly distressed as she arrived at the foot of the grand stairs. Susie and Max had scurried out of the kitchen into the foyer and the three of them just about collided right there.

Meg's face was white. The blood drained from her leaving her looking even more disturbed.

'Well, what is it Meg dear?' Susie demanded, her heart rate at an all-time high. So much excitement and it was barely 8:30am.

'Oh, my goodness, it's the worst possible news!' Meg cried out in despair. 'You will want to have me locked up I'm sure of it.'

Susie was puzzled by the distressed look on Meg's face. Sometimes she wished people would just get to the point and spit it out.

'Surely not. Is someone dead?'

Meg turned to face Susie with a look of astonishment. 'Dead? Heavens no, it's far worse than that!' Meg cried and ran off to the office.

Max looked up at Susie with surprise. What on earth could be worse than death? They both wondered hurrying after the distraught Meg. When they entered the office, they found her at the desk staring at the computer screen.

'I thought so. Oh, good lord no.'

'Now calm down dear and tell me what on earth is the matter and the cause of all of this commotion?' Susie reassuringly instructed her, taking a seat opposite her.

'It's the Aunties.' Meg finally blurted out. 'And they are coming for morning tea.' Meg double checked the calendar in Microsoft Outlook, and sure enough, it clearly showed the Aunties booked in for morning tea.

'Well, that is no cause for alarm Meg. When are we expecting them?' Susie asked sure it was not as big of a deal as Meg was making out with her youthful air of excitement.

'Now!' Meg said leaning back in the chair her hands covering her eyes. 'I am so sorry Ma'am, I totally forgot to tell you and to make arrangements for morning tea. What, with all the excitement of getting ready for your arrival, it clearly slipped my mind.'

'Well it doesn't seem such a big deal, I am sure we will rustle something up for them. I will see what Woolsworth can pull together if you like.' Susie was trying to calm the situation down. As far as she could tell there was no cause for such a fuss unless the Queen herself was joining them. 'Who are they anyway?'

'You don't understand Ma'am. The aunties are like local celebrities. And they are awful gossips, not to mention the fact that they have some influence around the town with the locals. The whole town will be waiting to see if they give the new resident of Ash Castle the thumbs up or the thumbs down.' Meg sighed and planted her head firmly in her hands, her elbows now resting on the edge of the desk.

'I see. Well, I tell you what young Meg. Who does the best catering job in town?' Susie had never been one to take the opinion of the local gossips to heart despite the fact she and Margery had done their fair share of gossiping. She did, however, see that there may be some advantage in having the thumbs up amongst the locals.

'Well, that would be Mr. McGill.' Meg said, her face brightening. 'Hunter McGill of the Famous Polmerton Bakery. He bakes the most delicious Hevva cake and whips the best-clotted cream in the traditional Cornish way.'

'Excellent. Why don't you take the Land Rover and hurry into town and see if this Mr. Hunter can help us out of this pickle?' Susie said. 'In the meantime, I shall change into something more appropriate to greet them on their arrival.'

'Terrific idea.' cried Meg leaping out of the chair, her mood somewhat improved. She bolted out the door leaping over Max as she went.

Glancing out from the balcony Susie saw a rather delightful old Bentley turning off the main road from Polmerton. Clearly, it was making its way to the castle. She had slipped into a more presentable pair of tweed slacks and a cream colored blouse which she felt was more suitable for entertaining guests for morning tea.

She made her way down the stairs to the foyer as the sixty-five model Bentley eased into the visitor car parking bay.

Swinging the front door open she watched as a rather fine looking young gentleman in a driver's uniform exited the driver's seat of the Bentley. He made his way to assist the Aunties from the rear passenger seat. Susie's glance lingering for a brief moment as he bent over to assist them.

The Aunties were Mabel & Mildred Milton. Twins, though they were non-identical. They were born the same year as Queen Elizabeth which put them at around 89 years of age. Despite their aging bodies, they were quick of wit and sharp as a tack. What's more, they knew everyone in town and were held in high regard by the town folk.

And as Susie was about to find out they loved nothing more than a good old-fashioned chat over a cup of tea and a little something.

Mable gave Susie a friendly wave as they made their way across the rather large car park.

'Brace yourself Ma'am,' Woolsworth sighed as he stood by Susie's side. 'Best I go polish the silverware,' he decided and turned on his heel to make himself scarce.

Mabel & Mildred made their way to the stairs leading up to the landing where Susie joined them.

'Welcome to Ash Castle.' Susie greeted them a little too formally.

'Oh, nonsense. We should be welcoming you,' joked Mabel, and they both roared with laughter.

'Seriously though a jolly good welcome to you, my dear, both to Ash Castle and our beloved Polmerton,' Mildred added.

'Well, thank you both.' Susie responded. 'I'm Susan Carter, but everyone calls me Susie.'

'Lovely to meet you dear, I'm Mabel, and this is Mildred.' Mabel said nodding to Mildred who nodded back. 'We are of course the Milton twins, but everyone calls us the Aunties. Not entirely sure why,' Mabel said with her thoughts drifting off.

'No. No one knows why they do really,' Mildred agreed and she also puzzled over it.

'Well, it's a delight to meet with you both.' Susie said as the three of them slowly ascended the steps to the front door.

A short while later they were seated in a large white rotunda with creeping roses behind the castle. It had a lovely outlook across a field bordered by stunning old oak trees. A disheveled greenhouse in the back corner was crying out for attention.

Susie had them all seated and instructed Woolsworth to make a giant pot of tea. Secretly she was praying inside that Meg had success with the bakery and was making haste on her return.

Small talk followed mostly about how Susie had settled in and what her old life in York was like. A few jokes about men, or the lack of them in Polmerton, had them all giggling like school girls. Max sat by Susie's side enjoying the happy banter.

'Now dear, a pressing question we have been dying to ask.' Mildred said turning a little more serious.

'Oh yes, what is it?'

'Well, we are not entirely sure if we should ask. Perhaps it's none of our business Mildred,' Mabel said looking at Mildred.

'Nonsense, I'm sure she won't mind sharing.' Mildred shot back a look at Mabel.

'Well, perhaps ask it anyway and see how we go.' Susie responded curiously.

'We were wondering what your plans are for Ash Castle?' Mabel jumped in.

'Oh, that is the question of the hour, isn't it?' Susie said. Truth be told, she had not given it a lot of thought since she had discussed with Meg the alarming financial situation. And it didn't look good. Susie had not yet had a chance to consider her options and devise a plan.

'We only ask because Charles was a dear old friend of ours. Known him for years, you know.' Mildred said with a hint of sadness in her voice.

'Such a shame really. He was a lovely fellow, and we did like to visit with him each week.' Mabel agreed. 'Of course, the matter is still something of a mystery as to what actually happened to him.'

Mildred glared at Mabel for saying too much. 'Well he was getting on a bit dear and his time was probably up!'

'Yes indeed. Never the less Charles had us up to date with everything, you know.' Mabel continued. 'It seems the upkeep of the castle ...'

'And the day-to-day running costs' Mildred added.

'Yes, and the running costs were all getting a bit too much for Charles.' Mabel finished fishing for information as to what Susie had in mind.

Susie looked at the Milton twins as they both stared back at her, eager to learn what might become of Ash Castle. On the one hand, she had no idea what she might do to get the Castle to cover its costs and perhaps even make a profit. On the other hand, she didn't necessarily want to tell them this as it would soon be the talk of the town she suspected.

'Well yes, I do have a few grand plans.' Susie said almost choking on the white lie.

'Oh, wonderful dear,' Mabel chimed.

'That's what we were hoping to hear' Mildred added. 'Go on let us hear everything.'

Inside Susie felt a sinking feeling. They were not going to let up until she had revealed every detail to them. But what on earth was she going to come up with on the spot that would sound half-feasible?

'Well, what I am planning is ...'

'Cornish delights!' a voice boomed across the pathway from the rear of the castle to the gazebo. 'Cornish delights for all!'

The three ladies all turned in unison to see a red-faced Hunter McGill wearing his baker's uniform carrying an oversized tray of traditional Cornish delights for the tea party.

Meg followed close behind with a plate of something delicious looking. Woolsworth reluctantly in tow with a fresh pot of Earl Grey tea.

'Here you go my lovelies' Hunter said placing the tray in front of the three excited ladies. He nodded at the Aunties who were old time friends. 'And you must be Lady Susan Carter. Delighted to meet you,' Hunter said taking Susie's hand and giving it a delicate peck. He beamed a warm smile at Susie which didn't go unnoticed by Mabel and Mildred.

Hunter McGill ran the 'Famous Polmerton Bakery.' Born and bred in Polmerton, Hunter was passionate about traditional Cornish style cooking. His bakery had won many an award over the years. He was somewhat rotund as a good baker should be, with ginger red hair and puffy red cheeks. His peaceful calm nature made him popular around town, and he was always on hand to chip in where he could help with local events and the like.

'Pleased to meet you Mr. McGill and thanks for getting us out of a pickle,' Susie smiled back at him. 'Won't you join us for a cup of tea?'

'It's a pleasure, and as much as I would like to I must be getting back to the shop.' Hunter said pleased to have had the offer. 'Hungry customers are waiting to sample the finest Cornish delights now.'

With that, Hunter said his farewells, smiled again at Susie and headed off back to work.

'Oh my, these scones with clotted cream are to die-for.' Susie said as pushed another laden with fresh local jam into her mouth. She had never tasted anything so delicious in all her life, and she was, after all, an experienced sampler of morning tea delights. She sighed at the joy of it and washed it all down with another cup of tea.

'Indeed yes,' Mabel said. 'Hunter is the best baker of traditional Cornish food in the whole of England.'

'Yes, it's a shame really he has never achieved the recognition he deserves for it.' Mildred agreed, and they both nodded in unison.

'That is a shame. He could make a nation delirious with delight.'

'Now, you were saying dear about your grand plans for the future.' Mabel said wanting to get back to business.

'Oh right, yes,' Susie was loading up another scone with Blackberry jam. 'Yes, big plans really.' She took a bite of the scone and realized just how much she loved to eat yummy foods.

The Aunties were all ears. On the edge of their seats. They waited patiently to learn every detail of the grand plans Susie had for Ash Castle. The truth was they couldn't wait to find out, so they could gossip around town, loving the idea of being first to bring the news to the village.

'Yes well, I have decided to start a traditional Cornish cooking school and run it right here at Ash Castle' Susie said a smile filling her face with the idea. She had no clue where the idea came from exactly, or how on earth she would make it happen. It just struck her like a bolt of lightning from the heavens above. But the idea sounded wonderful to her. 'Yes, and we will be teaching tourists how to cook traditional style Cornish fare.'

'You don't say?' Mildred said somewhat taken aback.

'What a terrific idea' Mabel said with great enthusiasm.

The Aunties nodded their delight at what a great idea it was. A cooking school would help to raise the necessary funds to ensure that Ash Castle was a going concern. And it had the added benefit of promoting tourism in Polmerton.

Woolsworth, who had been standing by in case he was needed, groaned his displeasure at the very thought of the great unwashed masses at the castle making a mess. He took the opportunity to depart muttering under his breath that if Ash Castle ever became a cooking school, the world would come to an end.

Susie sensed his displeasure, and it wiped the smile from her face. The idea had just popped into her head, and she had given it no consideration as to the details at all. Perhaps it was a bad idea.

'Now don't worry about old Woolsworth,' Mabel said.

'Yes, he is just bitter about how things turned out.' Mildred continued.

'Bitter?' Susie asked going in for her third scone.

'Oh, indeed yes the poor fellow. He was sure that Charles was going to leave the castle to him after so many years in service you know.' Mabel filled in the gaps.

'Seems he was quite put out when it was announced that he had no claims on the castle after all.' Mildred said sipping her tea.

Susie pondered this new information about Woolsworth. 'I see.' She said. Susie realized that the Aunties may be beneficial allies as far as finding out information was concerned.

'Now let's get back to more important business at hand.' Mildred said, keen to discuss the pressing matter of the cooking school.

'Yes, tell us more.' Mabel agreed.

Susie confessed she had not yet had a chance to give it a great deal of thought. It was mostly still on the drawing board, but the idea was taking shape as they spoke. They chatted back and forth discussing ideas on how a cooking school might work.

'Well it's a grand idea, and I do suggest that you enlist Mr. McGill's help.' Mildred said looking towards Mabel for confirmation.

'Oh yes he would love to help, no doubt,' Mabel agreed. 'Judging by the twinkle in his eyes just now.' They both roared with laughter. Of course, they fancied themselves as matchmakers, and this seemed a perfect opportunity to do some of their best work.

'What a wonderful idea. Do you think he might agree to assist?'

'Without a doubt, he would jump at the chance.' Mabel said.

'Of course, you will want to get the Mayor involved.' Mildred suggested.

'Well, that goes without saying' Mabel stated.

'The Mayor?' Susie asked.

'Well yes, Mayor Abigail McGill,' Mabel filled in the missing information. 'She is a great supporter of anything that will promote Polmerton. She will love the idea.'

'And don't worry dear. She is the ex-wife of Hunter, not the current.' Mildred said with a wink.

'Oh, perhaps she could make the keynote speech at the opening night.' Mabel offered, as an idea to which Mildred readily agreed would make sense.

'Opening night?' Susie asked with mounting concern.

This was all moving terribly fast for Susie. She had barely had a chance to get used to the idea that she and Max were to move from York to Polmerton, let alone running a castle and starting a cooking school with opening nights and Mayoral speeches.

4

A few days later Susie made her way to town to meet with Hunter McGill.

The idea of running a cooking school from Ash Castle and teaching tourists traditional Cornish style cooking had grown on her. Spending time on Google, she discovered endless local recipes that were in danger of being forgotten with the passage of time.

She reasoned that if she could do her bit to attract tourists to Polmerton, and at the same time preserve some Cornish histories, well it would be time well spent. Not to mention the most crucial item of funding the survival of Ash Castle.

As for the opening night party, she was still trying to muster the enthusiasm for it. She agreed with Meg however that it was essential to get the town folk on her side. So, a welcoming party might just do the trick.

At exactly three o'clock in the afternoon, she stepped inside the 'Famous Polmerton Bakery.'
Her senses were instantly overwhelmed by the abundance of taste bud delights on offer. Mesmerized by the cakes on display, she walked into a customer trying to depart with her purchases.

On hearing the brief commotion, Hunter McGill checked his hair in the mirror out back, straightened his freshly ironed shirt, and walked out to greet Susie. It was the best presented he had been in some time pondered Amiee, his shop assistant.

Susie glanced at Amiee who was thin as a rake and wondered how on earth anyone maintained such a delicate figure working amongst all these temptations.

'Lady Carter, an honor to have you visit us.' Hunter positively beamed with joy. His round red cheeks puffing up to match the color of his carrot top head.

'Please call me Susie, Mr. McGill,' she replied basking in the warmth of his greeting.

'Then I insist you call me Hunter!' he said in a jolly voice that boomed around the bakery.

'Well, that sounds reasonable Hunter,' she agreed and felt her own smile widening beyond its usual measure.

'Excellent. Then Susie, please come with me. We have lots to discuss.' He said, about to take Susie by the hand and lead her out to the courtyard in the rear where he had arranged a delightful afternoon tea setting for two.

Just as his hand reached out for hers, the door to the bakery burst open.

Hunter's mood instantly changed. Susie picked up on the energy but was unsure of the cause behind it. She turned around to find a slightly severe looking man filling the door frame.

At 53 and two years from early retirement, Inspector Reynolds filled the doorway with his bulking figure. An ex-heavyweight boxer and standing at 6'4" Reynolds was an imposing figure. His icy personality even more intimidating than his physical size. Town folk would often comment how they felt guilty in his presence despite if they hadn't a hair out of place.

'Inspector' Hunter nodded pleasantly, however, his tone of voice was full of venom.

'McGill,' the Inspector barely cast a glance in his direction to acknowledge him. 'And you must be Lady Carter I have heard so much about then?'

'Indeed, I am, and you are?'

'Inspector Reynolds, I keep things on the straight and narrow around town,' the inspector informed her rather pleased with himself.

'Well, not everything,' Hunter muttered sarcastically.

'Yes, and not every bakery has tried to kill me with a dodgy pasty, now have they?' the inspector was quick to reply shooting down any further attacks from Hunter McGill.

Reading the tense standoff Susie was quick to calculate that the two of them had some unresolved issues that had remained bubbling away under the surface. Later the Aunties explained that the Inspector had suffered food poisoning after eating a Cornish pasty he claimed he purchased at the Famous Polmerton Bakery. He was so ill he was unable to attend his own daughter's wedding the next day. Hunter denied it was one of his and they had been at loggerheads ever since.

'Well, pleased to meet you, Inspector.' Susie said nodding in his direction. 'Mr. McGill and I were just on our way to an important meeting, so I will bid you good day.'

'Before you go, Lady Carter, I need to discuss with you the unresolved murder of Charles Ash III.'

'Murder?' Susie was astonished. She was aware of some unexplained circumstances that surrounded his passing. But murder? She had not even remotely considered the idea of murder.

'Well, we are still trying to resolve this little mystery.' The Inspector said stroking his chin. 'Is it possible when you finish up with McGill here that you swing by the station for a quick chat?'

'Yes, indeed I will,' her voice trembling at the possibility.

'Good-oh then. I will see you a bit on. We're next door but two.' With that, the Inspector turned and headed out the door back onto High street. He turned right and walked the short trip to the police station to await her arrival.

Her mind was still swirling with the thought of murder when Hunter seated her out in the courtyard and poured her a welcome cup of tea. She glanced around the pretty cottage garden setting. One would never have suspected that such a haven would be hidden behind a bakery.

An eager Hunter passed a plate full of giant-sized scones her way. She chose the smallest one which was still larger than she thought she could get away with. Layers of fresh local jam and a dollop of clotted cream on top, just the smell alone was enough to get her salivating.

'Now then Susie,' Hunter said wiping cream from the side of his mouth. 'What is it you wanted to see me about?'

Susie had been wondering how to go about explaining the idea to Hunter. He was undoubtedly a busy man running the bakery and all. How could she enlist his help to ensure it was worth his time? She obviously did not want him to volunteer his services for free.

'Well, I need to enlist your services if you are willing.'

'Is this for the Cornish Cooking School you are planning at Ash Castle?' Hunter asked layering up another scone.

'Why yes, indeed.' Susie agreed somewhat amused. The Aunties are fast workers she joked to herself. 'You've heard about it then?'

'Oh yes. The whole town is buzzing with excitement.' Hunter winked at her.

'They are?' Susie asked taken aback that they would be showing any interest in her little project.

'Oh yes, they are. Not much excitement comes to Polmerton Susie, and this has everyone excited at the possibility.'

'Oh my, well, it's very much just the seedling of an idea.' Susie informed him trying to keep a lid on things until the seed had time to germinate.

Hunter opened his mouth wide in preparation for the incoming scone. Clearly, he was well practiced in the art of morning tea and scone eating. A chewed as he gathered his thoughts. 'Well, that's how all good things start. With the seed of a good idea.'

'I guess they do.' Susie laughed. 'The real question is how one takes a good idea and turns it into a going concern?' Back in York Susie had worked as the office manager for a law firm. She basically ran the day-to-day office functions of the business, but she hadn't the first clue on how to get a business up and running. Let alone how to start a cooking school. Or even how to teach cooking. Not to mention the fact that she knew little about traditional Cornish cooking.

All these thoughts had been swirling around her head for the last few days leading up to her meeting with Hunter.

'Well that is not a problem,' Hunter said. 'I will show you how and help you along the way if you like.'

'You would?' Susie was astonished at his generosity.

'Of course, my dear, and it will be a pleasure spending more time with you.' He smiled at her.

Susie blushed as she was sure he was flirting with her though it had been so long since she had flirted she wasn't sure she recognized the signs these days.

'That will be lovely. The real problem as I see it is I don't really know a lot about traditional style Cornish cooking.' Susie sighed, more to herself than Hunter. The lack of cooking knowledge seemed to be to big of a roadblock to moving forward.

With that, Hunter leaped to his feet and darted into the office behind the bakery. She could hear furniture being moved about the place. A moment later he returned with a thick manuscript in hand.

'Here it is,' he said and plonked the manuscript in her hands. It was dusty with a musty odor. Clearly untouched in many a year the print on the front cover had partially faded.

'What's this?' Susie asked curiously as she flicked through the pages containing old recipes.

'That be the history of Cornish fare,' Hunter proudly explained.

'You don't say?'

'Every traditional Cornish dish is listed with my grandmother's recipe. She got them from locals when she was a child. They don't come any more Cornish than what you will find in there.'

Susie was overcome with joy. This was going to fast track things, if she could get him to agree to let her use it.

'So, your family has been in Cornwall for some time then?'

'Oh yes. A good five generations or so,' Hunter said proudly. 'You wouldn't think so with a name like McGill. My great-grandfather made his way from Glasgow on a grand adventure and settled here in Polmerton. Never went back.'

'Oh well that explains a lot.'

'Yes, but sadly the Scottish name has held me back from getting the recognition my cooking deserves. Everyone who knows says it's the best in Cornwall.' Hunter said with a tinge of sadness. 'The Famous Polmerton Bakery is famous in name only.'

'Well perhaps with our new cooking school we can change all of that.' Susie smiled at him. She was sure they could work together and help each other achieve their goals.

'Oh yes. I'm hoping my grannie's recipes will see the light of day so any help I can offer I am more than happy to do so.'

The two of them chatted on for a good hour or so discussing all their ideas for the cooking school and how it might work. There were guest quarters at Ash Castle that could accommodate up to six couples. They could stay for a week and have an hour or two cooking class each day before sending them off to see the sites of the area. Then there was a good chance to run one day workshops and evening cooking classes as well.

They agreed that Hunter and Susie would become partners. All the proceeds initially going to get Ash Castle back in the black financially. From that point forward they would go halves in the profits.

Some discussion also followed about the big opening night to welcome Susie to Ash Castle and launch the cooking school to the local folks of Polmerton.

Susie bid him farewell with an excitement she had not felt since her teenage years.

As agreed Susie dropped in to see Inspector Reynolds.

The little police station was overcrowded with paperwork and filing cabinets. Lacking in ventilation and light, the small offices were dense with dust. The place needs a jolly good clean, Susie thought to herself as she took a seat opposite Reynolds.

He informed her that Charles Ash III death had some mystery surrounding it. Limited resources had meant he had yet to get to the bottom of it all, but he was confident that Ash met with foul play in the end. His aging years, however, had meant that most were happy to put it down to his time being up.

'So, what on earth makes you think someone may have had it in for my great uncle?' Susie said with some concern.

'Oh, Lady Carter, many a good folk around here had it in for him.' Reynolds said as he flicked through a file on his desk marked 'ASH III.' He found the letter he was looking for and handed it to Susie.

She paused a moment as she took in the contents of the handwritten letter. Then she sat back in the chair and crossed her legs, her mind going a million miles an hour.

'The letter was found in the side drawer next to his bed by Woolsworth,' Reynolds said indifferently.

'I don't understand, though.'

'Well, it's clear from the letter that someone was trying to blackmail old man Ash for a substantial amount of money.'

'That is clear. But who? And for what reason?' Susie gasped. Indeed, she could see why it was a mystery. What could someone possibly have over Charles that they would try to use it to blackmail him?

'What is unclear is whether he was forthcoming with the money?' Reynolds asked expecting Susie to have the answer at hand. Of course, she did not as she had not yet sat down with Meg to examine the books in detail.

'Well it would be a good thing to find out then,' Susie said with a blank look on her face.

Reynolds, not getting the response he had hoped for, discussed the matter with Susie further. He told her he would like her assistance in getting to the bottom of the issue, so he could close his file one way or the other. Foul play or not that was what they needed to resolve.

Agreeing to do all she could, Susie informed Reynolds she would make it a priority to examine every transaction in and out of Ash Castle accounts as soon as she could.

Pleased, Reynolds stood up and walked towards the door indicating the meeting was now over until they had more to discuss. Susie was eager to get out of there and back to the castle as fast as she could.

'Oh, there is one other matter,' Reynolds said as she was in the doorway.

'Oh yes, what is that?'

'Your neighbor, Douglas Hamilton, see what you can find out about him as well. It seems he was trying to buy some Ash Castle lands at some point, but they couldn't come to an agreement.'

Intrigued by the comment, Susie agreed she would report anything that seemed out of the ordinary to Reynolds. They bid each other farewell.

Susie headed back to the castle. Thoughts of her uncle meeting with foul play were quickly replaced with the excitement of her new partnership with Hunter McGill.

5

They stood together admiring how magnificent the grand ballroom looked all decked out for opening night. Meg sighed as she stood next to Susie, marveling at how much they had achieved in such a little time.

The grand ballroom had rarely been used in the past decade or so. Twenty years ago, it hosted balls and receptions for the people of Polmerton. Charles Ash was younger and loved to entertain. In more recent years as his health declined and age set in, his entertaining days came to an end rendering the grand ballroom without purpose.

With some hired help from the village, Susie, and Meg had given it a huge cleanup, and now it sparkled with delight. Everything was in order and for the first time in two weeks they had a moment to stop and get excited about the opening night.

Frequent meetings with Hunter ensured that they had planned both the menu for the evening along with advancing their plans for the cooking school. Hunter was getting about with more vigor in his step the Aunties mused. A new project to focus on and a potential new suitor they had laughed.

Susie, of course, was all business choosing to focus on the enormous task of regaining control of the finances of Ash Castle, holding a smashing opening evening, and creating the cooking school from the seed of an idea.

Instead of worrying about the pending financial storm about to engulf them, she had informed Meg; it was better to focus on what they could control with a positive can-do attitude.

And with that spirit, they kept themselves busy day and night for the past few weeks. The castle had not seen such a buzz of activity in many a year. Woolsworth maintained his less than cheerful demeanor the entire time, still protesting the very idea that his beloved Ash Castle should be turned into some cheap and nasty commercial cooking school for the weary masses.

Despite his constant and annoying objections Meg and Susie pressed on.

Now with the first guests scheduled to arrive in just a few hours, they stood at the entry to the grand ballroom and admired all they had achieved.

The rear wall now decorated with a giant banner that read "Cornish Cooking School—Polmerton," with the words "Welcome to the Grand Launch" scribed underneath.

The walls were lined with streamers reaching from the high set windows across to the center of the ceiling where a giant chandelier hung resplendent as the centerpiece of the ballroom.

Multi-colored balloons filled with helium scattered around the room with silk ribbon dangling down just in reach of the soon to arrive guests. Tables lined the walls gorgeously decorated and ready to present trays of the finest food Hunter McGill, and his team were busy preparing in the kitchens.

'Do you have the checklist there dear?' Susie asked of Meg.

'Check,' came back the reply to which they both giggled.

'So, what is left for the last minute?'

'The only item we are still waiting on is the lectern for the Mayoral speech.' Meg had informed her. They had discussed it with Woolsworth a dozen times, who kept promising to fetch it out of storage for them.'

'Well where on earth is that wretched man with my lectern ...' she was cut off in mid-sentence by Woolsworth groaning behind them as he made his way into the entry to the grand ballroom.

'Step aside Ma'am and make way for the wretched man if you don't mind,' Woolsworth said tersely. Susie's face flushed red with embarrassment. She wasn't one to speak ill of anyone and reasoned it must have been last minute nerves.

Woolsworth wheeled the lectern into place and wiped the dust and cobwebs from it. He presented it to the ladies with a gesture of his hands like he had watched one too many TV game shows.

Susie and Meg clapped in unison as the final piece was in place. Woolsworth took the opportunity to take a bow. Max barked three quick, delightful bark's joining in the fun of the moment.

'Now Ma'am, would you like the beast locked in the kennels where he will be out of the way?' Woolsworth tried again to get the dog out of the house. Susie was having none of it.

'Not on your life Woolsworth!' she said with authority and marched out of the room.

Right on six o'clock, the first guests started to arrive. Susie, Meg and Max formed a welcoming committee to greet each guest as they entered. This was, after all, a great opportunity to connect with all the towns folks and Susie was eager to make an impression.

The first guests to arrive where Mabel and Mildred, their driver pulling the Bentley right up to the stairs, so they didn't have far to walk. They decided to get there early so their driver could then take off early making room for other guests to arrive.

Mabel and Mildred stood with Susie to assist her by informing her who each of the guests were as they exited their vehicles. A temporary car park had been set up on the front lawn.

Everything was going fine when out of the blue a commotion started brewing in the car park. A larger-than-life woman was having a screaming match with an immaculately groomed fellow. It was becoming more and more heated with each passing moment. The woman involved started waving her hands around in the air and pointing a chubby finger in the direction of the immaculately groomed fellow.

'Who on earth is making that row?' Susie asked, somewhat saddened that the couple had chosen tonight to get into their marital disputes.

'Well, it looks to me like Mayor Abigail McGill.' Meg said with concern.

'Oh, quite right dear,' Mabel agreed, observing the commotion.

'And I do believe she is having it out with Heath Henshaw.' Mildred added.

'Good heavens!' Susie cried out in disbelief. 'What could they possibly have to fuss about?'

'Goodness knows' Mabel responded. 'Not aware of any troubles between them now are you Mildred?'

'What's that dear?' Mildred replied losing track of the conversation.

'Any troubles between the Mayor and Heath Henshaw that you are aware of?' Mabel asked again.

'Oh, no dear. Quite the opposite it seems they have a close working relationship.'

'Who is Heath Henshaw?' asked Susie.

'Heath Henshaw is an out of towner who settled her a few years ago. Property tycoon who has great plans for developing high-rise apartments along the harbor,' Meg informed her.

'Yes, but council so far has blocked his plans because they are unsightly and would ruin the very thing that makes Polmerton such a lovely spot.' Mabel added.

'Quite right dear and Mayor McGill is the one person on council who has the power to give the project the green light.' Mildred continued as the commotion died to a few muttered comments.

'And to date, she has not done so, costing Henshaw potentially millions!' Meg said completing the loop of missing information.

Susie was a little overwhelmed with all the new information she had just found out about Heath Henshaw. She made a mental note to make sure she spent some time getting to know Mr. Henshaw especially if he had a few million burning a hole in his pocket.

Mayor Abigail McGill made her way across the car park towards the steps leading up to the entry foyer. She gave the welcoming committee a friendly wave. At 5'11" and of a stocky build, and booming voice to match, she was a larger-than-life character. A fiery temper with street smarts to match, she had worked her way up from being raised on a sheep farm on the outskirts of town to be the Mayor of the city she loved.

Her rise to the top was not an easy one.

As the first female Mayor of the town, and indeed in Cornwall itself, she had to overcome a lot of the homegrown prejudices about a woman's role that still prevailed to this very day. At each step of her rise to power, she encountered men in influential positions who tried, in vain, to talk her down from the position she had risen to.

Now she was Mayor, she was not shy to voice her opinions about all manner of local business to the very people who foolishly tried to hold her back.

Polmerton had always been a progressive town by Cornish standards, and it was fitting that they should have the first female vicar and the first female Mayor. Fitting indeed that Susie had become the first female owner of Ash Castle.

Out of breath and with a bad back and knee, Abigail finally ascended the stairs and thrust her gloved hand in the direction of Susie.

'Lady Susan Carter! A delight to meet you at last,' She bellowed and sucked in air as her red face glowed in the dim light.

Susie went to shake the Mayoral hand and as she did, the light from the lantern caught the side of the Mayors face highlighting her forehead, nose and cheekbones on the right-hand side.

A chill went down Susie's spine and her whole body tensed. She gasped at the site. She let out a squeal of fright she hoped was only audible to herself, however, it was heard by all gathered at the front doorway.

Gathering her composure she clasped the Mayoral hand and pumped it vigorously.

'Pleased to meet you Mayor McGill and thank you so much for agreeing to attend and give a speech about our little venture tonight.'

'Oh, I am delighted to be invited,' the Mayor heartily replied. 'Such a great opportunity it will be for all of Polmerton.' Out of the corner of her eye, Abigail noticed that Henshaw had mounted the stairs and was about to walk past her, so she raised her voice, 'And one likes to do what one can to promote good business in town!'

Henshaw caught the emphasis on the phrase 'promote good business' and knew full well the comment was aimed directly at him. For the moment he chose to bite his tongue and continued into the grand ballroom in desperate need of a drink or two.

'Well, your generous support is most appreciated.' Susie smiled.

After exchanging a few more pleasantries, the Mayor excused herself pointing out she badly needed to pee.

Abigail entered the grand ballroom where people had started gathering.

Coming across the room was the last person she was hoping to bump into, but she figured if she was going to bump into him she might as well do it with style.

Hunter McGill was in his element, making his way through the growing crowd with trays of his soon to be famous Cornish Pasties. He whistled with joy, and he felt a good ten years younger. He hadn't noticed Abigail, coming straight at him. He did, however, feel the full force of her large frame. She was protesting that he was in the way as she made her way to the ladies.

'Excuse me do you mind not cutting me off and careful with those trays.' She bellowed at Hunter startling him, causing him to overbalance the tray. Pasties slid to the low end causing the center of balance to shift, and before he even realized what had happened, he had lost the load. His pride and joy upended on the polished timber floorboards with a splat.

Furious he glared at Abigail as she sailed by looking back over her shoulder to ensure she had the desired effect. Disappearing into the ladies, Abigail wondered how wise it was to finish the bottle of red she had an hour earlier.

He had finally had it with his ex-wife.

Bad enough that she made his life miserable during the three years of his marriage, more fool him in the first place.

And equally bad enough she had a habit of cheating on him. The final straw was when he came home and found her in bed with that slimy Douglas Hamilton.

And it was outrageous when she used her position as Mayor to block his plans for expansion of the 'Famous Polmerton Bakery,' even though the only reason she did so was out of spite.

But this! This was too much he thought to himself as he scraped the last of the mangled pasty's back onto the tray. Up since 4 am baking, with hardly any sleep, and fuelled by numerous coffees to wind him up, he went after her to give her a piece of his mind.

He was not accustomed to standing up for himself, but it was time to make a stand. She had made his life miserable one too many times. So, he stood waiting for her to exit the ladies.

'Now just what the bloody hell do you think you are playing at?' he demanded to know. It was the first time she recalled seeing him get mad enough to yell at her.

Never the less she was the Mayor, and as far as she was concerned, he was nobody; a plebe, an insignificant member of the public. So, she completely ignored him and walked back into the grand ballroom to mingle with her adoring public.

Outraged Hunter flipped out. Not wanting to make a scene he thought better of following her.

Instead, he did the next best thing and punched the wall so hard his fist split open in three places as he screamed 'That bloody woman I'm going to kill her!'

Jess Muller, the local preschool principle, exited the ladies at what proved to be the wrong time. On seeing Hunter McGill smash his fist causing a spray of blood to coat the white walls, and hearing him threatening to kill someone, she scurried back to the relative safety of her husband's side. Somewhat shocked at the scene she grabbed a champagne floating by on a tray and consumed it in one mouthful.

'Good heavens dear, you look like you have seen a ghost.' Mabel said to Susie after the Mayor departed for the ladies.

'Oh my, I thought I had.' Susie said as she took a vodka with lime from one of the waitresses handing out drinks. Not much of a drinker, she opened her mouth and emptied the contents of the glass in one movement.

The vodka hit her stomach and sent an immediate signal to the brain that it may not have been her smartest move for the night.

'What on earth is the matter?' Mabel pressed her.

Susie was too shaken up to speak. The image of the Mayor's profile lit by the exterior light had shaken her to her core. Indeed, she believed she must have just seen a ghost.

'Well, what is it?' Mildred joined in the concern.

Susie pointed towards the grand stairwell. At the halfway point stood, a life-size portrait of Charles Ash III decked out in his military service uniform and medals. His head cocked slightly to the right, the artist had perfectly captured the dim light of a lantern lighting his side profile.

Meg, Mabel, Mildred, and Max all turned in the direction Susie pointed.

They all instantly recognized the ghost that had put the fright in Susie.

Meg gasped placing her hand over her mouth to conceal any sounds of astonishment she may have made.

'Oh yes I see it, indeed' Mable said. Mildred nodded in agreement.

There, as clear as day, in the portrait of Charles Ash III they could all see the remarkable likeness to Mayor Abigail McGill.

Meg spotted Douglas and Laura Hamilton across the hall and thought it an opportune time to introduce them to Susie. She called them over hoping it would help Susie think about something other than ghosts and the like.

The Hamilton's were the immediate neighbors to Ash Castle. Douglas Hamilton's family had been in farming and owned hundreds of acres of prime farmland, much of which bordered the Ash property.

Douglas Hamilton always had an interest in real estate and property development. At a young age, he saw the growth in the Polmerton district. So, he opened a small real estate office, and quickly achieved success.

Of course, success had its perks. One of which was attracting the former beauty queen Laura Griggs. Laura was living in London and working for a fashion magazine at the time though she didn't really have the disposition for working. While returning on vacation back to Cornwall she made it her objective to track down a wealthy young suitor.

Meeting Douglas Hamilton at a local dance was her lucky strike. A whirlwind romance, followed by marriage, and she was soon moved into the country estate next to the old castle. For the most part, they had a happy marriage. She had pretty much everything she wanted and an easy life. As long as she could put up with his wandering eye?

'Doug and Laura, I would like you to meet your new neighbor Susie Carter.' Meg said. She enjoyed making the formal introductions.

'Well hello.' Susie greeted them, 'and thanks for coming along.'

'We wouldn't have missed it for anything.' Laura said. Susie noticed her eyes looking a little glazed and a slight hint of a slur to her words.

'Lady Carter, a pleasure to make your acquaintances.' Douglas piled on the charm taking her hand and giving a little bow.

'Likewise,' Susie said not entirely sure how to respond to such a greeting.

'I was very fond of Charles. He was a good man.'

'Oh, good to hear,' She responded. 'I didn't really know him that well myself, but from all accounts, he was a fine chap.'

'Indeed, he was.' Douglas agreed as his wife took another glass of wine and consumed its contents. 'When you have a moment Lady Carter, I would like to discuss with you some unfinished business Charles and I were conducting.'

'Certainly, why don't you pop over during the coming week for a chat?' Susie agreed. 'And please call me Susie.'

'Sounds excellent Susie,' he beamed a smile at her.

After exchanging some general chit-chat, the Hamilton's disappeared into the crowd to mingle with the rest of the town folks. There was a buzz in the grand ballroom and both the local wine and Hunter McGill's feast were proving to be a huge hit.

'Oh, here comes Councilor Bradshaw. Such a lovely chap' Meg said with delight. She recalled how kind he was to her when he would frequently visit Charles all those years ago. Back when she was just a child she remembered. 'He's quite a character. Let me introduce you to him.'

Meg waved him over to them.

He walked with a slight limp favoring the right side. He was delighted to see Meg once again and told her so as he gave her a customary peck on the cheek.

'Councilor Bradshaw, I would like you to meet Lady Susie Carter.'

'Nice to meet you Councilor,' Susie said offering her hand. He shook her hand politely.

'A pleasure to meet you too. I have heard so much about you.'

'All good I trust?' she joked.

'Mostly yes,' he played with her. 'But yes, such a marvelous thing you are doing to ensure Ash Castle is viable.'

Meg was keen to share with Susie how much of a castle enthusiast the Councilor was, but he beat her to it.

'I'm rather fond of the old castle you know.'

'Yes, Councilor Bradshaw is the local historian.'

'Oh, is that right? I would be keen to chat with you sometime.' Susie said. In the back of her mind, she had thought to find out more about the Ash family and their history with the town of Polmerton.

'Indeed, I am, though I rather have a love of the old castles in the Cornwall area, you know.'

Meg shared with Susie how Bradshaw was always over visiting with Charles a good ten years ago or more. The two of them spent hours together mapping out the old castle including the ruins in the eastern rear wing.

'You have a good memory then, my dear.' Bradshaw said to Meg.

'I would say besides the old man Ash and possibly Woolsworth you know the castle inside out better than anyone.'

'That could be true.' He had to agree with her. 'Yes, Charles had engaged my services to make detailed maps of every nook and cranny.'

'How fascinating, do you still have them then?' Susie asked thinking that the maps may come in handy at some point in the future. She hoped he had them safely stored away and would share them with her.

He thought about it for a bit. 'Yes, I believe they are in the filing cabinet in my office at the council chambers. It was some time ago though. Why don't you drop by sometime?'

Susie agreed that she would love to pay a visit and view the maps. It would be an excellent opportunity to find out everything she could about her ancestral history.

With that, Bradshaw spotted Douglas Hamilton and Heath Henshaw whom he had meant to catch up with to discuss some council matters. He excused himself and walked away. Susie watched as he walked away, thinking how difficult it must be to limp in such a manner.

Susie was lost in her thoughts for a moment before a little voice told her to snap out of it. She had a party to focus on, not daydreaming about old castles and history. There was more than enough time for that after tonight she thought.

'What time do we have dear?' Susie inquired of Meg.

'Oh heavens, its 7.21,' Meg replied checking her schedule. 'Not long before the Mayor's speech. I best go find her and get her ready then.'

Meg took off in search of Mayor McGill to ensure everything was in order for her keynote speech. Susie started to make her way towards the lectern in anticipation.

Meg searched for Mayor McGill for a good five minutes with little success. Finally, she stepped out onto the side patio of the grand ballroom which overlooked the grass field and in the distance spotted her talking to Butler Woolsworth.

As she approached, she noticed the Mayor a little unsteady on her feet. She was gesturing with some intensity. The closer Meg got to them the louder the Mayor's voice became. Woolsworth, however, was matching her intensity.

Goodness Meg thought they were having a heated discussion about something. She had no idea what this was about however she had caught them having a similar commotion a week before the old man Ash passed away. She wondered what on earth they could have to argue about?

Regardless, the show had to go on. She needed to get the Mayor away from this little confrontation and into shape to give the Mayoral speech. It was clear though this was going to be easier said than done as the Mayor appeared somewhat tipsy. She emptied another champagne glass.

'Excuse me Mayor,' Meg said, a little too meekly.

The Mayor didn't hear Meg and continued finishing her rant towards Woolsworth, 'You and I both know who the rightful owner is and who the old bastard should have left it all to!'

Meg tapped her on the shoulder 'Excuse me Mayor McGill,' she raised her voice to a level that she hoped might get the Mayoral attention.

'What on earth is it?' she turned and glared at whoever it was who would dare interrupt her. Realizing it was Meg, she quickly changed her attitude. 'Yes, dear how can I help?' she said with a smile that was somewhere between totally fake and relief.

'Sorry to interrupt Mayor. However, it is getting close to the time for you to give your speech,' Meg informed her. 'Everyone is so looking forward to what you have to say.'

'Oh yes, that!' Abigail remembered the primary purpose of her being there. She drained the last of her champagne, and the two of them walked back inside to the grand ballroom.

Susie stepped up to the lectern ready to start the formal part of the evening. Mayor Abigail McGill stood by her side with Meg and Max.

She switched on the microphone, and a shrill sound echoed around the ballroom startling everyone. The conversation which had been free-flowing wound down to a murmur as everyone recognized it was that time of the night.

Stepping up to the lectern Susie felt a tinge of nerves. She was not used to giving formal speeches as such, and she intended to make it brief and then hand over to the Mayor.

'Good evening everyone,' she said standing too close to the mic, her voice booming across the room. Abigail indicated to her to stand back a little which she promptly did.

'Good evening everyone from Polmerton.' She tried again. Everyone clapped at her welcome which helped her relax. 'I want to thank you all for such a warm welcome to your community. I am thrilled to be part of it and so excited you are all here for the official opening of the Cornish Cooking School to be held here in this very hall at Ash Castle.'

Everyone clapped, and for the most part, they all agreed that it was such a good idea for the town. Woolsworth rolled his eyes at the mention of the cooking school and departed the gathering in a foul mood. Old man Ash would turn in his grave if he knew what a debacle all this had become.

'I would like to introduce to you our special guest of the evening to say a few words, Mayor Abigail McGill.'

There was polite applause from some. Others murmured their displeasure for the Mayor, and there were one or two boo's amongst the gathering. Abigail took to the lectern with her usual flair.

'My good people of Polmerton,' she started with her canned opening for such an occasion.

With that, an extremely drunk Laura Hamilton made her way to the front of the gathered crowd. With a wine glass in one hand, she pointed her finger at the Mayor with the other and said 'Well at least some of us are good. You on the other hand, are not!'

The Mayor was momentarily taken aback by the wretched woman interrupting her.

Laura seized the moment 'How many more husbands here have you slept with?' she screeched at the top of her voice loud enough so that all and sundry heard. A look of sheer horror came across the crowd. 'Or was it just my husband you were sleeping with?'

Unsteady on her feet Laura knew she had everyone's attention, so she decided not to hold back. 'Did you do a deal with him, when you were sleeping with him, to ensure you got paid off as well?'

With that, Douglas Hamilton burst onto the scene and grabbed his wife by the waist and hurled her over his shoulder. He stormed out of the ballroom. Laura screaming obscenities as they went.

The Mayor was quick to regain control of the gathered folks.

'Poor dear, it seems the drink has gotten the better of her.' She joked, and everyone laughed with relief.

'Now, as I was saying. My good people of Polmerton, tonight is a historic occasion. Tonight, we not only welcome the new resident of Ash Castle, Lady Susie Carter, to our humble village, we also launch the start of her new venture the Cornish Cooking School.'

A round of cheer went through the crowd.

'Such a wonderful idea,' Abigail said turning to acknowledge Susie, 'Though I do think you could have picked a better business partner than that horrid ex-husband of mine.' The mayor joked. It was intended as a joke, and the crowd did laugh. Susie, however, was horrified and glanced across at Hunter who was still fuming from earlier. He stormed out to the kitchen not to be seen again.

'As Mayor of Polmerton, I do like to encourage what I term as, appropriate development for the community.'

'Unlike those terrible looking apartment buildings,' a voice hollered from the back.

'Yes, quite right. Any development needs to be appropriate and in keeping with what Polmerton is best known for. And that is why we are all so excited about this new venture here at Ash Castle.'

'Unless you get the percentage you demand.' Henshaw muttered under his breath. He said it loud enough for those nearest to hear, one of which was Susie. The Mayor herself heard the comment but carried on, regardless.

'I do hope that each of us will lend our support where we can to Lady Carter and the new Cornish Cooking School.'

Another round of applause.

'And now, it is with great pleasure that I officially declare the Cornish Cooking School formally open.'

A huge round of applause followed before everyone returned to their drinking and chatting.

Pleased it was over despite the challenges, Abigail excused herself and headed to the ladies.

Susie and Meg chatted with the locals many of whom came up to congratulate them on such an excellent idea. It was just what the old castle needed, and the town, to breathe new life into it. Everyone agreed that Susie would do exceptionally well with her new venture.

Jess Muller was lost.

She had enjoyed the evening immensely and had a few drinks. Now feeling slightly disoriented she searched for the hallway that led to the ladies. The old castle had some rather confusing corridors due to the various extensions added on over the centuries.

Taking a wrong turn, she walked in through the doorway to the pool room.

She screamed so loud it sent cold chills down the spine of all within hearing distance, which was most of the people still left in the grand ballroom.

The scream took her breath away, and she stood frozen on the spot unable to move.

The man leaning over the body stood up and looked at her in fright. He had blood on his hands as he turned to Jess to explain, holding his hands out.

Terrified she took off towards the grand ballroom screaming at the top of her lungs, 'He's killed her! He's murdered her.'

Jess ran to her husband where she promptly fainted in his arms.

Protesting his innocence, Hunter McGill had followed her into the grand ballroom where he now stood at the side entry door in full view of everyone. His hands and white shirt covered in blood, he cried out 'I didn't do it! I didn't kill her.'

Overcome with emotion and realizing how it must look he started to sob uncontrollably. He fell to his knees.

'Meg dear call the police and an ambulance, would you?' Susie said taking control of the situation. Meg ran off to follow instructions while Susie headed to the pool room to see what on earth had taken place?

She entered the pool room to find her laying on the slate floors, white in the face and surrounded by a puddle of her blood. Susie gasped with shock at the scene. Never in all her thoughts would she have guessed that Mayor Abigail McGill would wind up dead in her pool room, especially not after just giving her speech.

Mabel and Mildred had followed her into the pool room. They gasped in unison at the site of the dead Mayor. Barnaby Wellington, the local accountant and an emergency services volunteer, checked the body for signs of a pulse. Finding none, he stood back up and shook his head-no at the small gathered crowd.

The   Mayor   of   Polmerton   was   dead.

6

Confusion reigned amongst the guests still in attendance at the party. Some tried to leave, horrified at what had taken place. Susie overheard an old farmer comment that bad things had been happening at the castle ever since the first Ash moved in.

A group of folks, including Heath Henshaw, had gathered their coats and were making for the front door. On sensing their departure, Max leaped to all fours and ran ahead of them. He skidded at the entry and turned around to face them.

Henshaw tried to go around Max, however, he discovered it was futile. The fur on the back of Max's neck went up, and he bared his teeth as he snarled a warning.

No one was leaving until Max said so.

Alarmed, one of the ladies went to pat Max to make friends and then slip by.

Max was having none of it. He barked at her until she took a step back from the doorway.

Susie spotted Max standing guard and heard the noise he was making and rushed to the front door.

'I do apologize,' she stated, 'but I believe Max is right. No one is to leave until the authorities have had a chance to take a statement.'

'But I didn't see anything.' a voice protested.

'I saw that McGill with blood all over him. I'm sure he did it' Henshaw chimed in.

'Now let's not jump to any conclusions.' Susie said sternly. She couldn't imagine in her wildest dreams he would hurt anyone though at first glance it did look fairly damning for him.

'We're not jumping to conclusions. We all saw what we saw,' the voice replied and was met with hearty agreement. It was undeniable. The entire grand ballroom saw Hunter covered in blood chasing Jess Muller.

With that, they were interrupted by the sound of the local police vehicle rocketing up the driveway. Constable Daniels was at the wheel and determined to be the first on the scene.

At 23, Daniels was relatively inexperienced in such matters. Nothing much ever happened around Polmerton to get excited about. Laying on the couch in his boxer shorts he had been watching the first Ashes test cricket match between England and Australia broadcasting from the Gabba in Brisbane. The call came right at the moment when Flintoff was on a hat-trick.

Astonished by the nature of the call he was dressed, kissed his Mum goodbye and was out the door in less than three minutes. Motivated by the desire to be first on the scene, and the opportunity to see Megan Lane again, and maybe, just maybe he might pluck up the courage to ask her out sometime soon.

The gathering at the doorway watched as Constable Daniels abandoned the police vehicle at the foot of the steps and charged up them two at a time.

He arrived out of breath but eager to solve the crime.

Meg spotted his arrival and rushed over to greet him.

'Hello Constable Daniels.' She said coyly, 'and thank you for coming so fast.'

'Miss Lane, Ma'am,' he said acknowledging Meg and Susie.

Susie shook his hand relieved that someone in a position of authority was now on the scene.

'Perhaps you could take me to the crime scene.' he said to Susie.

'Oh yes of course.' She said before whispering in his ear, 'First though you might ask everyone to move back inside and that no one is allowed to leave until further notice?'

'Yes indeed,' he said giving her a smile of gratitude. 'Ladies and Gentlemen, I am sorry for the inconvenience, however, I am going to have to insist that you all move back inside until we have taken your statements.'

Pleased with his announcement he smiled again at Susie who smiled back at his efforts.

Meg applauded him for being so in control of things.

'Now this way,' Susie said and led Constable Daniels, Meg, and Max to the pool room.

At the sight of the dead Mayor, the young constable tensed up and gasped. He had never seen a real dead body before, and no amount of training at the Academy could prepare him for the reality of it.

The pizza and beers he had been consuming while watching the cricket now started to gurgle in his stomach. Nausea began to overcome him, and he started to dry reach. Sensing the pending situation, and wanting to protect the crime scene, Meg grabbed him by the arm and whisked him away to the men's room. Those left in the pool room listened on as the young Constable Daniels emptied his stomach in a series of ghastly vomiting episodes.

'Oh goodness, I do hope he is alright.' Mabel said having joined them in the pool room.

'She does look peaceful laying there doesn't she?' Mildred said staring down at the Mayor who remained motionless with rigor-mortise setting in.

'All right you lot, step away from the crime scene,' a voice boomed as it entered the pool room.

Inspector Reynolds, having been disturbed from his sleep, had come as quickly as he could. He was alarmed to find Constable Daniels had arrived on the scene before him. All he could hope was the young twit had not tampered with any of the evidence.

More guttural vomiting sounds echoed out of the gents.

'That Constable Daniels?' inquired Reynolds as he motioned for people to step back.

'Afraid so,' Susie informed him.

'Thought as much, no real-world experience just yet,' Reynolds delighted in telling them. 'Now if you could all step back and let me take a look.'

They did as they were told and stepped a good meter or two backwards.

Inspector Reynolds got down on his knees, and with a small pocket flashlight, he took a closer look at the deceased Mayor. He looked carefully at the wounds to the head and discovered that she appeared to have suffered not one, nor two, but three blows to the head. Anyone of them could have been the fatal blow. Which would indicate if this was a murder or a lesser crime, or possibly an unfortunate accident?

After all, it was obvious to Reynolds that she had been drinking, and a fair amount judging by the stench of alcohol that surrounded her.

'Any witnesses?' Reynolds said standing back up as Constable Daniels re-entered the room wiping his mouth with his sleeve. 'You alright son?' Reynolds inquired after his well-being. Daniels could only nod in reply, his face still white.

'One witness,' Susie informed him 'A Jess Muller says she walked in on the attacker who she says was covered in blood.'

'Okay, I will need to talk with her. You say she walked in on an attacker?'

'Yes indeed. Hunter McGill.' Mabel quickly added. Susie glared at Mabel wishing she hadn't been so quick to volunteer the information. She was after all convinced that Hunter was completely innocent of any wrongdoing, and time would prove her right.

'Hunter McGill hey!' the Inspector's eyes lit up. He had been waiting for an occasion to get back at McGill, and this was just perfect. 'Well, I shall have a little chat with the pastry man as well.'

Inspector Reynolds instructed Constable Daniels to take statements from everyone as to what they saw. He informed Daniels he wanted specific details and not just a bunch of vague nonsense. Daniels hurried off to follow instructions. Meg decided he probably needed her help and followed closely by.

'Inspector Reynolds, I do believe that Hunter McGill is completely innocent of any wrongdoing.' Susie explained to Reynolds.

'You don't say then?' Reynolds replied stroking his chin. He was going to enjoy putting the heat on McGill and make him wish he was burning in hell instead.

'Well, I just don't think he is capable of doing anyone any harm.' Susie pleaded with him to see reason.

'Lady Carter, please leave the police work to the proper authorities.' Reynolds objected. 'I am sure we are more than capable of getting to the bottom of what took place here.'

Jess Muller was huddled in the office being comforted by her husband. She had been sobbing uncontrollably and remained shaken up by what she had seen. Leading a somewhat charmed life, she had never encountered such violence and the waste of a life as she had tonight.

Inspector Reynolds entered the office and took a seat opposite them. Susie sat next to him with a notepad and pen in hand ready to take notes. She had argued the point with Reynolds that as it was her house, her occasion and her guests. She should at least be able to take a few notes. Reluctantly, and knowing it would spell trouble down the track, he agreed but swore he never would again.

'Ms. Muller, I'm Inspector Reynolds from the Polmerton Police Station.' Reynolds started out rather formally.

'Yes, I know that. Your grandson is in my flock, and I see you every Friday when you pick him up.' Muller reminded him. She called her students her flock and thought of them as being her own as she and her husband had failed in their attempts to get pregnant. It was obvious to Reynolds she was agitated at what he was now calling 'The Incident.'

'Perhaps you could tell me, Ms. Muller, what you saw?'

'It was horrible. He was dripping with blood.' Jess cried out. 'It was like he was on some killing orgy and he was eating her flesh or something.' Reynolds made notes. Susie was appalled at the description and interjected.

'Jess dear, it might be more beneficial for our inquiries if you stick with just the facts of what you actually did see.' Susie smiled and patted her on the knee. Reynolds looked up from his notepad at Susie trying to remember at what point in time it became 'our' investigation.

'Oh, I am sorry if I colored things a bit. I'm just a bit emotional that's all.'

'Understandable Ms. Muller,' Reynolds said attempting to show some empathy. He had been studying the 'Journal of Effective Policing' just last week when he came across a great article on the use of empathy. Tonight, he thought was a perfect time to test some assertions made in the article.

Jess gathered her composure. She handed her husband the last of the tissues she had used to wipe away her tears.

'I walked into the pool room accidentally as I was looking for the ladies. I often get lost in the old castle's hallways and the multitude of doors.'

'Yes, quite right.' Reynolds nodded in agreement and made a note.

'When I entered the pool room, I saw the baker ...'

'Hunter McGill?' Reynolds confirmed. Susie was sure she saw him smile when Jess agreed.

'Yes, that's him. I saw him standing over the body of the Mayor. She was lifeless and unmoving. A pool of blood had gathered around her head to one side. It looked like the side of her head had been caved in.'

'And what of Mr. McGill? What was he doing specifically?'

'Well, he was leaning over the body. He had his back to me, and he was bent over. When he heard me enter the room, he stood up and turned to face me. His hands had blood on them, and there was blood on his white shirt.'

'I see. So, he had the Mayor's blood on him then?' Inspector Reynolds asked sensing he was close to wrapping up the case.

'I am sorry Inspector, but there was no way she could know whose blood it was.' Susie interjected, feeling that way too many assumptions were being made, and conclusions being jumped to.

Reynolds gave her a cold stare and turned his attention back to Jess. He raised his eyebrows at her indicating she should continue.

'Well at that point I screamed, you know, at the sight of the dead body.' The memory of seeing the Mayor dead on the floor flooded back over her, and she wept again.

'And what did Mr. McGill do or say at this point?'

'Well, he protested his innocence. He cried out that he didn't do it, but to me, it looked as clear as the nose on the end of your face what had taken place. So, I screamed and ran back to the grand ballroom.'

'Did he follow?'

'Yes, he chased after me, and I feared for my life. I was worried I might be next on his list!'

'Rightly so, wise decision to run' Reynolds said and made detailed notes about the chase and additional threats to Jess Muller's life.

'Wait, a minute Jess. Is it possible that instead of chasing you, he too was running away from the scene that scared both of you?' Susie asked desperate to put a different spin on things to save Hunter from being trialed and found guilty right at this moment.

'Well, I guess it's possible.' Jess agreed but was quick to add that in her mind it was clear Hunter McGill chased her with the intention of making her his next victim.

'Seems like it's obvious what his intentions were towards young Jess here.' Inspector Reynolds said closing his notebook. He was all done with Jess Muller and keen to send her and her husband home for a rest.

'Am I free to go now?' Jess asked.

'Yes indeed, go home and get some rest.' Inspector Reynolds said with his best caring voice. 'We will need you to come down to the station tomorrow morning though to give a formal statement if that's alright?'

'Of course, Inspector,' Mr. Muller agreed. Frankly, he would have agreed to anything just to get out of there tonight Susie thought to herself.

Hunter McGill had been sobbing off and on since he was discovered standing over the body of his ex-wife. Now seated in the small dining area of the Kitchen, he was in a state of shock being comforted by his assistant Amiee.

Try as he might, he was unable to get the blood off his hands. It was not going to come out of his white shirt without a fight either.

He sat on a stool staring blankly at the floor trying to piece together what had happened. It all happened so fast. One minute he is passing the pool room when he hears the Mayor fall with a thud. He had presumed she had one too many drinks. Going to her aid, he noticed blood around her head. He bent down to check if she was okay. At that moment Jess Muller had walked in and shrieked.

'Oh, it doesn't look good for me.' Hunter said out loud to no one with his head in his hands.

'What doesn't look good for you McGill?' Inspector Reynolds asked as he entered the room. Susie followed behind. In her mind, she was sure that Hunter was not the violent type.

'Oh, Inspector, now I know what you think, but you must not jump to conclusions.' Hunter pleaded.

'I'm not entirely sure you do know what I think.' Reynolds replied. 'Just here to gather the facts as they pertain to your involvement in this murder.'

'Murder?' Hunter exclaimed. 'It wasn't murder, she fell and hit her head.'

'I see.' Reynolds made a note in his notebook.

'Now just start from the beginning and tell us what happened' Susie said in a reassuring voice.

'Okay, right you are. Well, I was walking past the pool room on my way to the gents. The door was open when I heard a loud thump and crash. So, I diverted into the pool room to see if everything was okay.'

'We have a witness that says she saw you standing over the dead body moments after you killed her! Inspector Reynolds Stated.

'Killed her?' Hunter was outraged at the suggestion. 'I didn't kill anyone!'

'So, what happened after you went to investigate the crashing sound?' Susie asked trying to ignore the Inspectors out of line questioning.

Hunter sat a moment and tried to recall the events. His mind was racing at the suggestion he might have killed Abigail. He had adored her. The love of his life until she broke his heart. Still, he would never want any harm to come to her.

'Well it was dark in the pool room; the light switch didn't seem to work. There was some light coming through the window from the half-moon though. I heard a creaking sound near the bookshelves like a door being closed. Over by the pool table, I saw a body laying still on the cold floor. So, I rushed over.'

'Did you know who it was at this point?' Susie asked. Reynolds gave her a why bother look. He had his man as far as he was concerned.

'Not until I got closer. Then I saw it was Abigail. I looked down, and she was still, so I bent over to try to help her up. I didn't know she had blood all over the floor and her head.' Hunter started crying again at the thought of his ex-wife laying dead on the floor.

Susie reached for a box of tissues on the bench and handed them to Hunter.

'So, the crashing sound was her falling?' Susie prompted Hunter.

'I assume so. She had a fair bit to drink, and I assume she fell and hit her head on the slate floors.'

Inspector Reynolds was having none of this. 'Not your place to be assuming anything now, McGill. Now tell us what the murder weapon was that you used to kill her?'

'Weapon? There was no weapon as far as I know.'

'Right, you just pushed her over then did you?' the Inspector pressed harder going for a confession.

'I did no such thing!'

'Well, would you mind telling us the nature of your relationship with the deceased then?' Inspector Reynolds asked waiting for Hunter to slip up and give him the key piece of information he needed to lock him away.

'You know damn well what my relationship with Abigail was.' Hunter said, holding himself from screaming at the Inspector.

The Inspector made some notes on his notepad about the witness being reluctant to co-operate with the investigation. 'Yes, however, for the record, we need to hear it in your words. So, what was your relationship with the deceased?'

Hunter McGill gave a detailed account of his rocky relationship with Abigail McGill. He explained in detail, causing himself much anguish, how he had come home one day to find her in bed with Douglas Hamilton.

'So, it's clear you had a strong motive for murder then?' Inspector asked.

'Maybe in your twisted mind, Inspector but not in mine,' Hunter retorted.

Susie decided it was time to steer things back in a more reasonable direction. 'So, after you found her what happened next?'

'Well as I was trying to say, I bent over to help her up not realizing she was dead. That's when my hands became covered in blood. At that point, I heard someone enter the room. I stood up and was about to ask the person to get help when she screamed at the top of her voice that I had killed her.'

'And do you know who that person was?'

'Well, I assume it was Jess Muller. She was screaming that I had murdered Abigail and of course I had done no such thing.'

'You do realize Mr. McGill that we will get to the bottom of this. Better you tell the truth now.' Inspector Reynolds stated.

'Yes of course and I am. So, she is screaming murder, and I was in shock, I didn't know what to do. As she ran out yelling to all and sundry that I was the murderer I ran after her ...'

'Chasing the poor woman to shut her up then?' Reynolds said with glee. This was going perfectly. It was his chance to once and for all nail the fat man from the bakery whose pasty had made him so sick he missed his daughter's wedding.

'I wasn't chasing her. I was going to get help. I ran into the grand ballroom where everyone turned and stared at me. I realize it must have looked bad at that point' Hunter said, his head now resting in his hands as he recalled the devastating moment.

'Well, I think I have heard more than enough McGill. You will need to come to the station tomorrow to give a formal statement. In the meantime, don't leave town.' Reynolds said. It was getting late, and as far as he was concerned, this was a closed case he could wrap up tomorrow after a good night's kip.

Meg had shown the Forensics team to the crime scene. As luck would have it, the lead investigator was her older cousin Emma Swallow. The two of them had always got on famously, so it was such a relief to Meg to see her smiling face.

The Forensics department was based in Newquay where they covered all the Cornwall region.

Emma and her team set about examining the crime scene. They dusted the entire pool room for fingerprints and took numerous photos of the body to be used later in their investigations.

Inspector Reynolds and Susie joined Emma in the pool room.

'Any updates?' the Inspector demanded.

'Well at this stage, not a lot to go on.' Emma said, 'Looks like she has three blows to the head here, here and here.'

'Yes, that's what I was thinking.'

'Clearly, she had a lot to drink as well by the smell of alcohol.' Emma continued. She was not a fan of getting drunk at public events. Sure, one or two drinks but not fall down drunk.

'We found a small sample of hair and skin on the edge of the pool table.' Emma added holding up a small sample bag. 'Indicating that she probably hit her head.'

'So, it's possible she may have just fallen, hit her head on the pool table, and then again on the slate and died from an accident.' Susie said with hope in her voice.

'Well, that would explain two of the blows to her head certainly.' Emma agreed, which left the matter of the third head wound hanging. 'We will know more when we get her to the lab and conduct a proper investigation.'

'Right you are then.' Inspector Reynolds said. 'Seems like we are ready to wrap things up here then.'

Emma and her team bagged the body and wheeled it out into the waiting ambulance for transfer to their crime lab.

'Got a statement from all the main players then?' Inspector Reynolds asked the young Constable.

'Yes, Inspector I certainly have.' The constable was proud of his work lining everyone lined up and taking their statements. Meg smiled at him for having done such a good job.

'Right then Lady Carter, it seems like we are ready to finish things up here. We will send everyone home. Are you going to be alright here on your own?'

Susie was still processing the events of the evening and not really tuned in to what the Inspector was saying. The last of the guests left. She felt sad as she watched Hunter McGill get into his car and drive away. The evening had shown such promise for better things to come, but now it all just seemed to be such a mess.

'Lady Carter?' the Inspector interrupted her thoughts.

'What? Oh yes, I will be fine. Besides, I have Meg here, and Max to look after me.'

'Right-oh then.'

The Inspector motioned to the Constable it was time to take their leave and head home for the evening. Meg leaned across and gave Constable Daniels a quick peck on the cheek and squeezed his arm. His face flushed bright red with embarrassment, and he nearly tumbled down the stairs. He didn't mind though. It was a good night of police work, and she was finally starting to notice him.

'Oh my, what a night,' Susie said to a weary Meg in the Kitchen later. They sipped a small glass of port each, trying to unwind. Both exhausted from the weeks-long build up to the opening night, and of course, the events that unfolded.

'You can say that again. I do hope that Mr. McGill is found innocent after all,' said Meg.

'Well, I for one believe he wouldn't harm a fly. I am sure the Mayor just fell, and it was all an accident.' Frustration set in on Susie's face though. It was obvious to her that the Inspector had it in for Hunter, and he was going to try to pin a murder on him without proper investigation.

'Yes, he has such a pleasant nature normally, though he did seem to be in a bit of a mood earlier.'

'I suspect it was just the stress of getting everything ready for the arrival of all of our guests.'

'Yes, I imagine so.' Meg drained the last of the port from her glass. She had drunk more than she would normally and felt ever so tipsy. She walked over to Susie and wrapped her arms around her and kissed her on the cheek. 'I am so glad you are here now. Good night.'

'Good night dear.' Susie replied with a chuckle. She watched young Meg head off to bed and wondered how anyone could sleep with all that had taken place.

Susie sat up and went through the events of the night discussing it with Max. He listened with great interest and cocked his head to one side when she made valid points.

It did look bad when Hunter arrived in the grand ballroom covered in blood and seemingly chasing Jess Muller. Her screaming 'murder' only added to the scene. And no doubt he had something of a motive even though being left by your wife is hardly the strongest of motives of all time.

Deep down though she felt she had had the chance to get to know his nature, and it seemed unlikely that in the heat of the moment he had it in him to commit such a horrible act.

She decided that she must get to the bottom of it before the Inspector ruined his life, which he seemed determined to do.

7

The next morning Susie was up and about early. She had a restless night with little sleep. Her mind going over and over the events of the evening trying to make sure she didn't miss any vital piece of information that might point to the real killer if indeed there was one.

Bright and early she took Max for a walk into the woods behind the castle. Ash Castle sat on approximately twenty acres of prime real estate high on the hill overlooking Polmerton and the ocean.

Gorgeous woodlands on the side of the hills offered excellent bushwalking and were a challenging workout that she and Max both enjoyed. One had to walk off all those scones she would tell Max each morning.

Max, of course, loved a good walk and relished the opportunity to sniff every tree, and chase the odd rabbit into the scrub. Susie and Meg would spend hours pulling the burrs out of his thick coat in the evenings as they watched TV together.

On ascending to the peak of the hill where the view was at its best, she looked down on Ash Castle below, and further to Polmerton. All her troubles at once seeming smaller and less significant. A different perspective on things always helped as her grandmother was fond of saying.

On her return to home base, she showered and dressed ready to head into town. She had made up her mind she was going to discuss the events of the night with the Inspector first thing.

She was certainly not happy that he was so quick to convict Hunter without due process.

She arrived at the police station as Inspector Reynolds was just turning the old key in the door.

'Inspector Reynolds, I am glad I caught you first thing.'

'Morning Lady Carter, and what can I do for you today?' he asked as he swung the large door open. Switching on the lights revealing the dust laden office he walked across to his desk and dropped his briefcase on the floor. Susie followed him and took a seat opposite his desk.

'Well, I wanted to discuss the events of last night with you.'

Inspector Reynolds leaned back in his old leather chair and crossed his legs. He stroked his chin and stared down the length of his nose at Susie wondering what she was playing at. 'Seems a closed case to me. I'm just waiting on forensics before we go ahead and book McGill with murder.'

Susie was not surprised he was taking such a narrow view of the case. His life would be easier, and it would be better for the whole town, to have this wrapped up as soon as possible.

'Yes, I understand, however, have you considered others who might have an even stronger motive for committing murder, if in fact, it was murder?' Susie asked, the tone of her voice quite insistent.

'Well Constable Daniels took statements from everyone and we shall be reviewing those in due course.' The Inspector offered.

'Yes, of course, however, let me run through a list of people you might want to discuss the matter with further? I have been going through the events of last night and it seems to me that several people may have a potential motive.'

Inspector Reynolds sighed. He could see she wasn't going to let up until he had at least discussed her list with her. No doubt she would demand that he go and speak with each of them. Not what he wanted this close to his retirement; he was counting the days down and with just fourteen months to go, the last thing he wanted was a lengthy drawn out investigation into anything.

He leaned forward on his desk and retrieved a fresh notepad and pen.

'Right-oh then. Let me have the list?'

'Oh yes well, the first person you should speak with is Laura Hamilton. It seems she caused a scene right before the Mayoral speech accusing the Mayor of having an affair with her husband.'

'Was she drunk?'

'I beg your pardon?' Susie was taken aback by the question.

'Was the woman drunk at the time of the scene?'

'Yes, I do believe she was somewhat intoxicated.' Susie said wondering now if it was just the drink talking.

'Yes, I suspected as much. She's a shocking drunk and always makes a scene at every public event.' The Inspector informed her.

'She does?' Susie couldn't believe anyone would subject themselves to the level of embarrassment she would feel if she herself had caused such a scene.

'Quite right she does. The poor woman is desperately trying to get the attention of her husband. That sort of behavior is what we have come to expect of her.' The Inspector put his pen down realizing that this was probably going nowhere.

'I see. Well, perhaps you should also discuss the matter with a Mr. Heath Henshaw. He was seen having a huge disagreement with the Mayor earlier in the evening. I hear that the Mayor had blocked his plans to develop apartments in town.'

'A fender bender,' a voice came from behind them. They both looked up to see young Constable Daniels arriving for work and joining in the conversation.

'What's that constable?' Inspector Reynolds asked for clarification.

'The disagreement between the Mayor and Mr. Henshaw. It was a fender bender. I asked Mr. Henshaw about it.'

'Go on then.'

'Seems that Mr. Henshaw was upset with the Mayor for having cut him off in traffic on the way to the event. He had words with the Mayor about nearly hitting his 78 Jaguar.'

'And?'

'And according to him the Mayor was already rather under the influence of alcohol and flew into a royal rage at him.' The Constable filled in the details.

The Inspector nodded to the Constable for a job well done. He then turned and fixed his glare on Susie. He was growing increasingly frustrated with her.

'Anyone else on your list Ma'am or are we free to get on with real police work now?' the Inspector asked with a sarcastic snarl.

'I just don't think Hunter could have done it, and I am certain you have yet to complete your investigations to be jumping to any conclusions.' Susie said and thumped his desk.

'Ma'am with all due respect, I suggest you leave the police work to us.' Inspector Reynolds said firmly. 'There is new evidence that has come to light that you are not privy too. Evidence which firmly puts Hunter McGill as the guilty party.'

Reynolds went to stand up to encourage Susie to do the same, ending the conversation. She was having none of it.

'What is the new evidence?' she insisted. Reynolds sat back down. He wasn't aware of any new evidence, he was just trying to get this painful woman out of his office. He turned to Constable Daniels in the hope he had some.

'Oh yes indeed there is some new evidence.'

'Well, what is that then?'

'Jess Muller, when I spoke with her, she says that earlier in the night Hunter McGill got into an argument with the Mayor. He was later seen to be punching his fist into a wall and screaming out ...' the Constable thumbed through the pages of his notebook. 'Words to the effect of, I am going to kill that woman.'

With that, the Inspector stood up and with his hands motioned to the door. As far as he was concerned he was ready to arrest McGill now and it would be his pleasure to do so.

'Well, that is hardly sufficient evidence. That is more like hearsay!' Susie cried out raising her voice.

'For goodness' sake woman, the man threatened to kill her and shortly thereafter he is seen standing over her dead body covered in blood. He had as strong a motive for murder as any I have seen in thirty years. I dare say if he didn't do it then it will go down as the greatest murder mystery in the history of Polmerton.' Inspector Reynolds had become animated and red in the face as he made his point clear.

'Well, I insist he didn't do it. He is innocent until proved guilty, and I am going to hold you accountable to following due process. Good day to you!' Susie said storming out of the police office.

Susie called Meg into the office and closed the door behind her.

'Meg, am I right in remembering that the head of the forensics team, Emma, is a friend of yours?' Susie inquired.

'Oh, more than a friend. She is my first cousin and was my best friend growing up.' Meg's face lit up at the thought of childhood memories at the beach with Emma. The two of them in their bright pink swimsuits and bonnets.

'You don't say?'

'Why do you ask?'

'Well, I was wondering if you felt like paying her a visit. See how her investigations are getting on?'

Meg explained that her cousin worked out of the office in Newquay which would be a good fifty minutes drive. They discussed the trip and if they felt Emma might help Susie with her inquiries. In the end, they thought it was worth the trip to find out.

Just under an hour later they were standing at the modest entry to the forensics laboratory in Newquay where Emma and her assistant worked.

Meg tapped on the glass pane of the side door. On hearing the knocking at her door Emma appeared in a full gown, face mask and surgical gloves. She had been right in the middle of the examination of the body of Abigail McGill when she saw the car of her beloved cousin coming down the street.

'Oh, I hope we are not interrupting anything then?' Meg exclaimed.

'Not really love, I was just finishing up.'

Emma led them into the office area and gave them a seat. She departed for about ten minutes to clean up and get changed. On her return, she brought with her a lovely tray full of pots of tea and some jam tarts baked fresh this morning.

They all enjoyed themselves making small talk for a bit before Emma finally asked, 'So I guess you have come to find out where we are up to then?' Emma smiled as she asked it knowing full well this was more than a social visit.

'Yes well, we were curious indeed?'

'Well, there is not much to tell, really. It all seems a bit of a routine case of a whack across the head and she fell down dead.'

Meg shuddered at the thought of poor Abigail being whacked on the head.

'Do you think the first blow to the head is what killed her then?' Susie questioned.

'Definitely was. She was dead before she fell and hit her head. Firstly, on the pool table, and then on the slate floor accounting for all three blows to the head.'

'And did you ascertain a time of death?'

'Yes, the exact time of death was 8:11 pm'

That is a good forty minutes after she finished her speech Susie thought to herself. What on earth happened during those forty minutes? And she was sure that Hunter McGill didn't appear in the pool room until at least 8:25 pm.

'Tell me Emma, a big pool of blood on the floor. How long would that take to dry?'

'If there was enough blood, then anywhere from 10 minutes to thirty minutes; depends on the temperature of the room and how much blood there is.'

'So, it's possible someone who found the body after about thirty minutes could still wind up with blood on their hands then?'

'More than possible.' Emma agreed. 'However, as it dries, it tends to darken. If we found some on clothing, for example, we could tell how old it was when it soiled the clothes based on the coloration.'

'Oh goodness' Meg shuddered again.

Susie's mind was pondering this new information. It's possible that the Mayor had been dead for at least fifteen minutes when Hunter found her. So, from the time she finished her speech, there was a window of about an hour where anything could have happened.

'And what do you think may have caused the initial fatal blow to the head then?'

'Oh, that looks like a metal object, either a golf putter or a fire poker. Did they find a murder weapon of any description?'

'None that we are aware of,' Meg answered.

'Thank you Emma, you have been most helpful indeed. And thank you for the tea.' Susie said.

They said their goodbyes and Meg and Susie returned to Meg's Rav 4. They buckled up and were about to depart when Emma came running out of the house waving something in the air at them.

Meg stopped the car and turned off the key.

Emma had run around to Susie's side of the car and was waving a sheet of paper at her as Susie opened the passenger side window.

'What is it dear?'

'I almost forgot to give this to you.' Emma said out of breath. 'I found it in the Mayor's pocket scrunched up into a small ball.

Susie took the sheet and examined it in detail.

'Looks like it was the Mayor's speech all typed out.' Susie said reading it over.

'That is what I thought. This part is interesting.' Emma said pointing to a line that had been crossed out in blue pen.

Susie read the line.

'We are pleased to welcome the new resident Lady Susan Carter to Ash Castle, despite the fact old man Ash had promised to leave it all to me!!!!'

'Oh, good heavens!' Susie was shocked as she thought about the crossed out line. Why would Charles have promised to leave the castle to Abigail McGill she wondered? Or was it intended as a joke?

On the drive back to Polmerton they discussed the fact that a single blow to the head killed the Mayor. They went over the events of last night and agreed there had been no concerted effort to locate a murder weapon that either could remember.

They decided that as soon as they got home they would turn the castle upside down in search of every metal object that could have possibly created a blow to the head such as the one Abigail had received.

After a slow drive back home, Meg parked the car around the back in the large garages reserved for staff.

Woolsworth was nowhere to be seen. Meg was not alarmed by this as he often took an afternoon nap and was usually up by 5pm for the evening activities. On checking, she found his bedroom door closed and the rhythmic sounds of snoring could be heard reverberating around the room.

Max had been waiting for their return. He was asleep on his mat in the corner of the small dining room of the Kitchen. On hearing Susie's voice, he jumped up and dashed into the Kitchen, his tail at a fever pitch of excitement. His excitement was justified as he got a prolonged pat and scratch from both Susie and Meg. Susie found him a treat which he promptly took back to his bed to devour.

For the next hour, the two ladies turned over practically every corner of the downstairs living areas in search of a potential murder weapon. They started in the pool room where the closest they came were the pool cues in their racks. They were specifically looking for a metal object, however, as Emma had pointed out. They had found a small amount of cast iron in the initial wound.

Having no joy in the pool room they moved to the Kitchen and turned it upside down. Susie realized that in the shock of it all last night Hunter had left behind a considerable amount of cooking utensils which she vowed she would return to him tomorrow.

Next the Grand Ballroom. Every nook and cranny were searched. They were chatting at the tops of their voices and making a racket when a weary looking Woolsworth appeared in the doorway.

'May one inquire as to what all this is about?' he asked fearing he would be the one to have to clean up. He knew the party and the cooking school were going to be nothing but trouble.

'We are looking for a murder weapon' Meg responded.

'Yes, something along the lines of a fire poker.' Susie added hoping to inspire Woolsworth to join in the search.

'One would imagine if one wanted to find a fire poker then one would look where there was a fire to poke!' Woolsworth said tersely and walked off. At times he forgot his place in the pecking order. Susie ignored his rudeness however as he had made a fine point.

'To the lounge room,' Susie shrieked and the two ladies ran into the oversized lounge room which contained enormous wood fire place's at either end of the room. Two fireplaces meant two sets of fire utensils.

They checked the first and everything appeared to be in order. They ran the length of the room and checked the second set of utensils. The fire utensils were made from cast iron and hung from a stand next to the fireplace. A small broom, a dustpan, and space where the fire poker should be hanging.

'Oh, my goodness!' Meg screamed.

'It's missing!'

Meg and Susie decided there is a high chance that it had been hidden by the culprit to conceal key evidence. If only they could locate it.

8

Frustrated at the lack of a murder weapon following their big search the night before, Susie awoke the next morning and decided she had to take matters into her own hands. If she left it to the authorities to discover who the culprit was, then she feared that poor Hunter might not get out of this mess.

Considering all the events of the evening she made a list of people she might pop in on and make some inquiries with.

Her first port of call was to be Heath Henshaw. Sure, the young Constable had said the fight he was having with the Mayor was over a fender bender, but she was sure there was more to it than that.

After breakfast, she asked Meg to find the address for Heath Henshaw. A moment later she came back into the dining room with his business card. Meg explained that he had dropped over to visit the old man Ash a month or so before his passing. Thankfully, the card had the office address for Henshaw Developments. Susie headed into town.

Susie walked along the harbor side of the road admiring the view on her way to Henshaw Developments. Polmerton sure was a pretty town she thought to herself. Small fishing boats and yachts bobbed up and down in the harbor swaying gently in the breeze. At high tide, the harbor was a magnificent site. As the sun came up, it sparkled across the still water of the harbor. Despite the recent tragic events, Susie felt alive and grateful for the opportunity given to her.

Arriving at the office of Henshaw Developments she opened the door and set off the buzzer. The small foyer had a reception desk and comfy leather recliner for visitors to wait.

On hearing the buzzer, a rather beautiful young lady walked into the reception. She was immaculately groomed in a suit, comprising a rather short skirt and silky pink shirt. She stood several inches taller, thanks to the high heels she was wearing. Her long flowing blond hair swished stylishly about the place.

Susie was impressed by how impeccable her styling was but noted that she looked entirely out of place in a town like Polmerton. She struck Susie as being the type to work in a stock brokerage firm in London's financial district.

'Good morning Ma'am. May I help you?' She inquired. Beautifully spoken as well, Susie thought to herself.

'Yes, good morning dear, I am here to see Mr. Henshaw.'

'And do you have an appointment?'

'Well no. I didn't think I might need one. Just a quick chat is all.'

'I will see if he is available.'

With that, the immaculate blond walked off into the back of the office in search of Henshaw. Susie glanced around at some photos on the walls of the office. Pictures of development projects completed by Henshaw Developments she thought to herself. And in all honesty, they looked rather impressive.

'Lady Carter, to what do I owe the pleasure?' Henshaw's voice oozed with charm as he entered the reception.

'Oh, good morning Mr. Henshaw. Wonder if I might have a quick word.'

'Certainly, come with me.'

Henshaw led her through the back offices and into a large boardroom. Spread out on the boardroom table were large architectural plans for what looked like an apartment building development.

Susie walked over to the plans and started examining them.

'Impressive isn't it?' Henshaw asked.

'Oh, very much so. Such a grand vision.'

'Yes, well we thought with the likelihood of a new Mayor coming in, and most likely a change of attitude towards development in town, that it might be time to revise these plans.'

'Yes, indeed it makes sense'

'Smashing party, the other night too.'

Susie was not sure how to respond to his enthusiasm for her opening night party. In her mind, it was anything but smashing. More like a total disaster.

'Oh, you enjoyed yourself then?'

'Had a wonderful time,' Henshaw said with delight. He realized that perhaps it was not the most appropriate thing to say under the circumstances, so he added 'I mean notwithstanding the untimely passing of our beloved Mayor. Apart from that it was a wonderful night.'

'Oh, good to hear.'

'Now to what do I owe the pleasure of your visit?'

'Well, I wonder if I could ask you a couple of questions. Perhaps of a sensitive nature if that is alright?'

'Yes of course. I have nothing to hide. Ask me anything.'

'Thank you. I just wanted to ask you about the disagreement you had with the Mayor on your arrival to the car park the other night?'

'Oh, how do you mean?'

'Well, a good number of people heard you and the Mayor going at it in the car park. A rather heated exchange.'

'Oh, that. It was nothing really. The Mayor was obviously in a hurry to get to the party and cut me off in traffic, almost hitting my beloved Jaguar. I had simply suggested she watch where she is going in the future.'

'And how did she respond?'

'Quite surprising really. That's when I assumed she had drunk too much. She flew into a rage.'

'A rage?'

'Yes, she started screaming and yelling at me about all manner of things. I let her cool down and then made my way to the party. She was fine after that. Why do you ask?'

'Oh well, it seems the authorities want to pin the murder of the Mayor on Hunter McGill without a thorough investigation of what took place. So, I thought I might make a few inquiries of my own.'

'Quite right to do so, though he did look like the guilty party when he appeared in the doorway covered in her blood. We were all in total shock at the site.'

'Yes, I imagine so.'

'Is there anything else I can help you with?'

'No that was all I wanted to know' Susie said. After chatting on briefly, Henshaw led her back to the reception to bid her farewell for the day. She had her hand on the doorknob when she turned back to Henshaw.

'Mr. Henshaw, may I ask before I leave, what exactly was your relationship with the Mayor?'

'My relationship? Well, I didn't have a relationship with her as such. I had some dealings with her a few years ago when we tried to get the Harbor Apartments through the council. She was opposed to it all, and that was about the end of it.'

'I see. Well, good luck with relaunching the project then.' Susie smiled and said goodbye.

Such a charming man she thought to herself. And everything about him, his office and the staff were just so perfect. Not a hair out of place. So, unlike most of the old salty sea dogs, she was used to seeing around town.

The office of Hamilton Real Estate was across the other side of town. She walked through the small village and peeked in at all the shops. She was starting to recognize some familiar faces here and there which made her feel at home.

On arriving at Hamilton Real Estate, she was shown into a meeting room to wait for Laura Hamilton. She flicked through some property magazines while she waited. A short time later an argument broke out in the small kitchen next to the meeting room.

It was clearly a man and a woman having a heated argument but trying to mute their voices so as not to be heard by everyone in the office. Susie peeked through the small crack in the door and saw Douglas and Laura Hamilton clearly not happy with each other.

He stormed off, and Laura pulled herself together before joining Susie in the meeting room.

Laura Hamilton was an attractive lady at 46. Her face showed the signs of having a lot of stress in her life, but she had maintained her figure and looks from her youth. As a teenager, she pursued a modeling career in London but thought better of it and chose to stay in Polmerton with her childhood sweetheart Doug. Together they had started Hamilton Real Estate, and she had been the office manager ever since.

'So nice of you to visit us, Lady Carter.'

'Thank you dear, and thanks for taking the time to see me.'

'I must apologize for my outburst the other night. I suspect someone must have slipped something in my drink.' she laughed, a fake laugh that wasn't convincing even to herself.

'Oh, that is quite alright dear. Good thing Mr. Hamilton rescued you when he did, I suspect.'

'Oh, I barely remember a thing. Just remember him tucking me into bed before he went back to the party. Now, how can I help you?'

'I wanted to just get to the bottom of a few things.'

'Yes of course.'

'You know the authorities have Hunter McGill clearly in their sites for the murder of the Mayor.'

'Oh, not dear Hunter. Did he do it? I mean he probably had reason to!'

'I don't think he had anything to do with it personally, and yes a good many people perhaps had reason to do it.'

'I imagine so. She was a horrid woman.'

'This is a little delicate to ask, but I understand your husband had some liaison with the Mayor at some point?'

Laura rolled her eyes and folded her arms. She sighed, searching for the words to explain the situation.

'If by liaison you mean affair then yes. He did have an affair with the cow.' Laura said becoming agitated at the thought. 'But it was a once off affair, and he said it was all about business!'

'What business?'

'That dreaded apartment building with Henshaw.'

'Your husband was involved in the proposal for the apartment building?'

'Yes. He and Henshaw were partners. Dougy put up a large chunk of our money for the project. And he would have been the selling agent for the apartments.'

'Oh, and what happened?'

'All the council was in favor, but the Mayor blocked it sighting some ancient piece of legislation, something about preserving the historical nature of the village or some such nonsense.'

'I see.'

'Truth was the cow just wanted a payoff for her stamp of approval.'

'How much?'

'A million pounds she asked for.'

'Good heavens!' Susie said astounded at the news.

'Yes, quite right. The project had hardly any margin, anyway. The only reason we were doing it was to bring more tourism to the town.'

'Very good of you.'

'So Dougy was meeting with her over drinks to try to talk her around.'

'And that's when the affair happened?'

'Yes, I believe so.'

'That must have been hard on you poor dear.'

'Yes, a shocking business really. Totally embarrassing to have the whole town know about your life.'

'So, how was your relationship with the Mayor from that point forward?'

'I wanted to kill the cow of course.' Laura said matter-of-fact. 'But I just avoided any contact with her. She tried to see me to explain, but I wanted nothing to do with that money grabbing whore.'

Susie was shocked at the language but felt it was justified considering. She watched as Laura looked away and stared blankly at the floor. Behind those eyes, she knew there was a lot of pain and anguish that she had not yet fully resolved.

'Well thank you for your time.'

'McGill killed her I am sure of it!' Laura said without looking up.

'Why do you say that dear?'

'I bumped into him not so long ago. We chatted briefly, you know, both being the victims of their affair, and he was still so angry she had left him for Dougy.'

'I see.'

'He had said something along the lines that she was trying to destroy his business as well, and he would kill her if he had the chance.'

'Good heavens!' Susie was astonished at the allegation. 'That doesn't sound like the Hunter I know.'

'Well, there is no telling what a person is capable of when they are finally pushed to their limits now is there Lady Carter?' Laura said making eye contact with Susie with an intensity that was unnerving.

'I guess not dear, no.'

After saying farewell to Laura Hamilton, Susie walked back through the village in the direction of her car. She was going over the conversations in her head piecing together what she had learned.

Lost in her thoughts as she turned around a corner she bumped directly into Inspector Reynolds who wasn't watching where he was going. They collided with a thud knocking Susie of her feet sprawling across the footpath. He was a solid fellow indeed she thought.

'Ma'am, are you okay?' the Inspector asked helping her to her feet.

'Oh yes perfectly fine. Apart from the embarrassment,' she said straightening her skirt.

After checking she was in fact okay, the Inspector took the opportunity to have a word with her.

'Lady Carter it has come to my attention that you have been meddling in police business of late and I want to suggest, that you leave police matters to the police.'

'Good heavens, what on earth do you mean?'

'Well I was speaking with Emma of forensics, and she informs me you had visited her. Now you really must not be interfering, or you could set our investigations back.'

'Social visit.'

'A what?'

'It was a social visit Inspector. It turns out Emma is the cousin of my Meg. They hadn't seen each other in a while and decided to catch up for a cup of tea and a chin wag.'

'And you just happened along?'

'Well, Meg was kind enough to invite me, show me the countryside and so on.' Susie said. She flashed the Inspector a generous smile knowing full well he couldn't stop anyone from paying a friendly social visit.

'Well just stay out of our way. I also saw you leaving the Henshaw office as well!'

'Oh, I wasn't aware that Mr. Henshaw was part of your investigations Inspector?'

'No one is above suspicion Lady Carter.'

'Does that mean your case against Hunter McGill is not looking so solid after all?'

'Not at all no. I am sure we have our man.'

'Really?'

'In fact, I am just on my way back to read the forensic report to confirm it is a murder we have on our hands.'

'And if so?'

'Then I suspect we will be placing Mr. McGill under arrest!'

'You cannot be serious Inspector. On what evidence do you have?' Susie demanded to know. She was fuming as she knew the Inspector had convinced himself of Hunter's guilt for personal reasons more than sensible police work.

'Well, he was seen at the scene of the crime Ma'am, you know that. People saw what they saw, and it was plain as the day is long.'

'All circumstantial Inspector, no witnesses saw Hunter McGill involved in anything other than cooking and serving of food.'

'Yes, but he clearly had a strong motive. Still, bitter about his dispute with the Mayor.'

It was clear to Susie that she was not going to get the Inspector to see reason at all. Not when he had his star witness Jess Muller so eager to testify to Hunter's guilt. The only way to change his mind was to identify key evidence that will lead to the real killer.

But where to start?

Her chats with Henshaw and Laura Hamilton went nowhere. She was unsure of what to do next and decided she must chat with her old friend Margery and seek her counsel on the matter.

Arriving home Susie popped into the office were Meg was busy filing paperwork from the opening night party.

'Oh, where have you been then?' Meg asked with a giant smile warming the room.

'Having a bit of a chat with a few of the townsfolk,' Susie replied. 'Would you do me a favor dear?'

'Of course.'

'Would you do some research for me on Google and see what you can find on Jess Muller. Any sort of background information might be useful.'

'I most certainly will. I will get on to it right away.'

'Thank you dear.'

With that, Susie wandered up to the master suite. Max, glad she was home, followed her. If there was to be an afternoon nap, then he was more than happy to partake.

Susie sat in the recliner on the balcony and dialed the number for Margery.

'Hello, my dear it's me.' Susie said. Relief at the sound of her old friend's voice came flooding through her body. The last few weeks had been a whirlwind of life-changing events, and with the murder and all, well she was feeling quite emotional. Fortunately, she was sure that Margery would not mind all her blabbering and emotions that had built up.

'Now dear take a deep breath and start at the beginning. Tell me everything.' Margery said with a calmness that always helped Susie to relax.

Thirty minutes later Susie had caught Margery up with all the events of the opening night, and the murder of the Mayor.
She expressed her frustration at the Inspectors determination to pin the murder on Hunter.

'So, tell me again dear, what evidence does the Inspector have on this Hunter chap?'

'Well, none really. Hunter was seen standing over the body, there was blood on his hands and shirt. Earlier he had been heard to say he would kill her which seems out of character.'

'And all of this evidence originates from one key witness then?'

'Quite right, yes. A Jess Muller says she overheard the threat to kill earlier in the night and then found Hunter standing over the dead Mayors body.'

'Well, that seems a bit farfetched to pin someone as a murderer on the say so of one witness. She didn't even see the murder take place.'

'No, she did not.'

'And has the Inspector identified a motive?'

'Yes, that is where it gets a bit murky, really.'

'How so dear?'

'Well, it seems Hunter McGill was married to the Mayor Abigail McGill.'

'Oh, is that so?'

'Yes, and he came home one night to find her in bed with a Douglas Hamilton who just happens to be my neighbor.'

'Oh no, the poor chap this Hunter.'

'So, Inspector Reynolds believes that this is a sufficient motive.'

'Oh never. If you ask me, it sounds like this Inspector has it in for your good Hunter.'

Susie marveled at how perceptive Margery is. She had the unique ability to read between the lines and grasp the true essence of what is going on in any situation. As friends, they would watch every episode of Miss Marple on TV and Margery would solve every crime before the final ad break of the night.

'I do think you are right.'

'Well, there is only one thing to do then dear.'

'What is that?'

'He only has one witness that he is building his case on. If you find something to discredit her testimony, then he has nothing.'

'You are a genius dear,' Susie said thanking her for her kind ear and suggestions. Of course, Susie had already been thinking along the same lines. If Meg could dig up anything from Jess Muller's past that would make her testimony less credible in court, it would surely help Hunter's case.

9

'This strawberry jam won't come out of my wretched shirt!'
Hunter shouted from the little wash-up area in the back of the
bakery. His assistant went to look to see if she could help.

That morning Susie had decided to check in on Hunter and
return his things he left behind at the party. He spotted her and
wandered out into the shop.

'How are you today?' she asked with concern in her voice.

'As good as can be expected I suppose.' Hunter replied still
distracted by the sticky jam situation.

'What is the problem with the jam?' Susie inquired having
heard him complaining when she walked in.

'Oh, that wretched strawberry jam is still stuck in my shirt.
Blood red it is but sticky as all get up.'

'How did you get it on your shirt then?'

Hunter explained how at the opening night party he had
raced back from his car with a tray of strawberry Jam Tarts that he
had forgotten to get earlier. As he ran up the back steps, he had
tripped and landed in the tray covering his shirt in the sticky mess.

'Oh no. Try some bicarbonate of soda. That's what my
mother always used in such situations.' Susie suggested.

'Will do.'

'Hunter, I wanted to chat with you about Inspector Reynolds.
It seems he has it in for you and is keen to pin the murder of the
Mayor on you.'

They chatted for a while about how the Inspector had always
had a dislike for Hunter. For some reason, Reynolds was always at
him trying to find fault, or make fun of him, or just generally bully

him around. Hunter agreed that having missed his daughter's wedding was a big deal indeed. However, it appears that the dislike had been going on for some time before that.

'I've meant to ask you.' Susie said. 'You knew Abigail as well as anyone. Who do you think might want to do her in like that?'

'Good question. And why wait until the night of the opening party?'

'Oh, an equally good question, I hadn't considered that.'

'Well, the problem is that Abigail made a lot of enemies along the way. She stepped on toes, did things her way and made life difficult for a good many folks around town.'

'So, it could have been any one of a number of people then?'

'I guess so if you only look at motives. There were a good few of us with what you might consider strong motives.'

Over the next twenty minutes, they went through and made a list of everyone he was aware of that had ever had a grudge against Abigail. The list totaled eleven people that he knew of including himself.

Of those eleven, several were no longer in town, and two others were out of town on holiday in Scotland at the time. One deceased leaving five possible suspects. The five remaining suspects being Heath Henshaw, Douglas Hamilton, Laura Hamilton, Councillor Bradshaw and Joe Spencer.

Susie had met Councilor Bradshaw at the opening night however she was not familiar with Joe Spencer. She made a note to chat with both as soon as possible. No one had seen or heard of Joe Spencer in months which ruled him out.

At that moment the door to the bakery burst open like it had been kicked off its hinges. The bell, designed to announce the entry of a new customer, flew from its hinges and slid across the tiled floor. The doorway filled with his bulk as Susie's heart sank.

'Hunter McGill, I am here to inform you that you are under arrest for the murder of Mayor Abigail McGill.'

Susie gasped. She had to hold herself back from screaming. She protested at the lack of evidence and the injustice of arresting Hunter without following through with a complete investigation.

'Lady Carter, I believe we have already discussed you not interfering with official police business, have we not?'

Inspector Reynolds glared down at Susie giving her a look that would freeze the Sahara Desert. In no uncertain terms, he was making it clear that she should back off.

'But you don't have any evidence linking Hunter to the actual murder, that's if there was one!' She protested anyway. She was not going to give up without a fight. And Hunter was worth fighting for. Besides the fact, he was a nice chap, and she believed he was innocent, she needed him for the Cornish Cooking School. Without him, it couldn't go ahead, and the future of Ash Castle would be under question.

'Well, I can confirm that the Mayor was indeed murdered. The forensics report is now in, and she was killed with the first blow to the head. So, it is in fact, a murder, not an accident.'

'Yes but ...'

'And Mr. McGill here was found by a key witness standing over the body shortly after the crime took place.'

'And what time was that exactly?'

Inspector Reynolds checked his notes. He had a look on his face of a man wondering why he was bothering to answer such questions.

'The specific time of death according to forensics was 8:11 pm.'

'Well, in that case, it couldn't have been me!' Hunter piped up in his defense.

'And why is that then?'

For the first time since this whole mess began Hunter was feeling confident that common sense would prevail, and people would realize he had nothing to do with it. Now upon hearing the time of the murder he knew that they would not be able to make any charges stick.

'Well, you see I was here at 8:11 pm on the night.'

'You were?' Susie asked with surprise.

'How is that then if you were at the party all night?' The Inspector demanded to know. He wasn't going to allow Hunter McGill to fool him around, but he would at least hear him out on this.

'At about 7:45 we realized that all the deserts were going at a great rate of knots. Everyone seemed to love my grandmother's secret recipe for fluffy scones and clotted cream.'

'Yes, get on with it then!'

'When I was informed that they were nearly all gone, I went in search of the Strawberry Jam Tarts. Four large trays of them and I knew that everyone would just love them, so I saved them for last.'

'And?'

'And I went into the Kitchen to fetch them, that's when it struck me. I felt rather foolish, and I'm ashamed to admit it, but I left them all back here at the bakery.

'So what?'

'Well, I headed back here to the bakery, loaded my car up with them and departed back to Ash Castle at precisely 8:20 pm. You see Inspector I was here at the time of the murder, so I am afraid you have the wrong man.'

'I will determine that.'

'Well it seems obvious, Inspector, that it couldn't have been him.' Susie drove the point home but to no avail.

'And what time did you arrive back at Ash Castle then?'

'Approximately 8:27 pm. I had finished unloading my car when I heard a crashing sound in the pool room and went to investigate.'

'Did you indeed?'

'Quite right yes, and that's when I found her on the floor. I tried to help her up, but she was well dead by then.'

'And that's when your so-called witness arrived on the scene,' Susie added, trying to drive the point home.

'Oh aye, and what proof do you have that you were here at the time of the murder then?'

Hunter hung his head defeated. He had no proof, and he realized it was his word which may not be held in high regard given the witness had earlier heard him threaten to kill her.

'None I'm afraid,' he muttered.

'I thought as much then.'

The Inspector put away his notebook and pen. He looked at Susie to see if she had anything further to add to the conversation. On receiving nothing, he finally got to do what he had been longing to do for some time.

'Hunter McGill, you are under arrest for the murder of Mayor Abigail McGill. Anything you say can and will be used in a court of law. You have the right to remain silent.'

Inspector Reynolds continued reading his rights to him as the young Constable Daniels motioned for Hunter to turn around. He placed the cuffs on his wrist but rather kindly didn't do them up tight.

The two police officers then led Hunter out of the 'Famous Polmerton Bakery' and down the street to the police station where he was formally charged with murder.

The small police station had one lock up with a reasonably comfortable bed and a color TV. Thinking better than to protest too loudly Hunter decided to take a nap and then catch up on some of his favorite TV shows that he didn't have a chance to watch regularly.

With Hunter locked up, Susie instructed the bakery shop assistant Aimee to look after everything for a few days. At least until Hunter was released. Aimee readily agreed. Susie knew that she would do an excellent job.

Susie wrote her phone number down on a piece of paper and handed it to her. 'Now if you need anything at all dear, then you give me a call right away.'

10

The Aunties had arrived promptly at 3:00 pm for their usual weekly tea with Susie. Susie herself was not long back from the bakery. She was still in shock that poor Hunter had been arrested and she vowed to sort things out and see to it that he is released as soon as possible.

Fortunately, Meg had already organized afternoon tea. She had bossed Woolsworth around to get everything in order which he complained about bitterly. One of the qualities that Susie loved about Meg was that she thought ahead and stepped in to help when needed.

A short time after their arrival, Mabel, and Mildred were seated in the garden rotunda with Susie, Meg and Max. Woolsworth poured tea all round and frowned at young Megan Lane for joining the tea party. He had an excellent mind to remind her that she was after all just the hired help and not a member of the tea party itself.

Susie had insisted that Meg join them, however. She enjoyed her company, and it softened the full force of the Aunties.

With all the stress of Hunter getting arrested and the murder at the party, Susie had been feeling a touch out of sorts. Her disposition changed however when she spotted Woolsworth bringing a rather large tray of delicious scones their way. She dove in, eating several in a flash knowing she would regret it when they found their way to her hips, but deciding to have another, anyway.

'Oh dear, that's quite an appetite you have there,' Mabel said making light of Susie vacuuming up the crumbs on her plate.

'Poor Susie, she has had a lot to deal with lately.' Meg jumped to her defense.

'And what is the latest on the murder investigation then?' Mildred asked Susie.

'Yes, we hear Mr. McGill has been taken into custody by the authorities?' Mabel added, the pair of them, staring at Susie for the answers.

'Well yes indeed the Inspector did arrest him just a few hours ago.' Susie sighed. 'But I am sure he had nothing to do with it.'

'We think the Inspector is just out to get Mr. McGill.' Meg said with a tone of disbelief.

'You don't say?'

Susie and Meg brought the Aunties up to speed on the highly circumstantial nature of the evidence against Hunter McGill. They discussed the fact that the Inspector was relying almost entirely on the hearsay of one witness.

Mabel brought up the issue of motive and questioned if Hunter's motive was strong enough to have killed his ex-wife. Mildred was quick to suggest that he had adored her and was broken-hearted when she left him, however, he would never hurt a fly let alone kill anyone.

There was unanimous agreement that it couldn't possibly be Hunter, and the police had it all wrong.

'So, what has Hunter had to say in his defense then?' Mabel asked.

'Well, Hunter says that at precisely the time the murder took place, he was in fact back at the bakery in search of some absent Strawberry Jam Tarts.'

'Oh, I do love those.' Mabel smiled at the thought.

'Oh yes, when it comes to Strawberry Jam Tarts he cannot be beaten.' Mildred readily agreed.

'They were rather delicious.' Meg had to add with a smile.

'Yes, they are, however, he has no proof he was at the bakery at the time, so the police just think he made it all up.' Susie said layering clotted cream onto her third scone. She looked at Max who was giving her a knowing look that they would be doubling up on walks for the rest of the week. He didn't mind as a pleasant walk in the woods with his master was without a doubt one of his greatest delights in life. He gave her a smile and an enthusiastic wag of his tail.

'Why don't you check the CCTV footage then?' Mabel asked without much thought.

'That's a thought,' Meg chimed.

Susie nearly choked on her scone. She was so upset about the police taking him away that she wasn't thinking clearly. It hadn't occurred to her that there may be footage from a nearby camera or two. And now Mabel just popped the idea out without giving it much thought.

'Yes, I am sure the Smugglers Inn would have cameras mounted outside that would pick up the bakery.' Meg said after giving it some thought.

'Quite right, it's just a couple of blocks away after all.' Mildred said.

Susie and Meg decided they would visit the Smugglers Inn immediately after the tea party concluded.

The Aunties inquired as to when the first official cooking classes where to be held at Ash Castle. Susie informed them of the plans to start running them at the beginning of June when the weather was on the-improve. As it was only six weeks away, they all prayed Hunter would soon be released so he could focus on helping her get everything in order.

'Such a shame about Abigail though.' Mabel sighed.

'Oh, she was deep down a decent person you know.' Mildred said recalling some good work the Mayor had done for charity.

'I wonder if anyone had contacted the poor girl's mother.' Mabel said.

'She has a mother?'

'Oh yes, she does. They have her in a home though as she started losing her mind about five years ago. She has not been the same since.'

'Yes, that's right. She is at the Ocean View Home in Carnon Downs I believe.'

'Indeed, you are right.'

With the scones, all cleaned up, and the teapot drained several times, Woolsworth swooped in to clear the mess. The sooner he could get this little tea party wound up the sooner he could get to his afternoon nap.

Satisfied that they had a jolly good time, the Aunties kissed and hugged both Meg and Susie. A few extra pat's for Max, and they were on their way.

The moment the Bentley wound its way down the driveway Susie and Meg gathered their belongings to head out themselves.

The Smugglers Inn was built in 1781 and was one of the first buildings in Polmerton besides Ash Castle. At the time it was built, there was a harbor with a few small boat sheds. The only industry was fishing.

It was built by an Irish man named Fergal Barrett. He had sailed across from Cork when he heard the stories of the great Cornish mining boom. Knowing full well that one thing miners do well is drink, he and his two sons set about building the Barrett Inn & Boarding House. It provided a bed for the night, a pint of beer and a good feed to the local fishermen, and miners.

It remained as Barrett Inn until thirty years ago when its name was changed to Smugglers Inn as part of a big Cornwall wide tourism drive. Sadly, it didn't drive a lot more people in the doors, but the new name had stuck.

The Smugglers Inn remained a local's pub to this day. An aroma of fish and salty sea dogs filled your nostrils on arrival. It had many of the original fittings in it including a large stone fireplace with wooden mantelpiece. The timber was said to have come from a mast of the ship 'Landsworthy' local legend claimed was sunk by pirates just off the coast.

Perhaps the most distinctive feature of The Smugglers Inn was at the rear. At some point in the last few hundred years, a rather large hall was added to the back of the old pub for the performance of theatrical plays. It seated a hundred or so people with a small stage and area for the performers to prepare behind the stage. It was rarely used today except for the annual Pirates and Wenches Ball.

Meg led Susie into the pub suggesting she duck her head through the low doorway. A visual feast, Susie took in as much of the unfamiliar scene as she could. A moment ago, they had been standing out in the light of the day observing the location of the CCTV cameras.

Now in the dimly lit front bar of the pub, Susie, and Meg struggled to have their eyes adjust.

'Young Megan Lane. Not often I see you around these parts love!' a voice called out with the sweet melody that only the Irish seem to have.

It was the voice of the Innkeeper Patty Malone, as Irish as they come, Patty had been born and bred at the Smugglers Inn. Her parents came across from Ireland forty-two years ago when they inherited the pub. She was born there, and it became hers when her dad passed away two years ago.

'Oh hello, Patty. I want to introduce you to Lady Susan Carter.'

Patty leaned across the bar her large hand offered as a welcoming gesture.

Susie shook her hand and smiled.

'Well, this is quite a place you have here.'

'Aye, you could say so.' Patty said glancing around the pub with its smattering of locals and a family of American tourists loudly eating their lunch in the corner.

'Now that's quite a stir you have been making up on the hill there.' Patty joked with them. She laughed a hearty laugh at the thought of all the commotion at the old castle.

'Oh yes, I am indeed sorry about that,' Susie said feeling a tad embarrassed.

'No need.' she laughed again.

Meg got down to business. She explained the murder that took place and the fact that Hunter McGill was arrested for murder. She went into detail about the time of the murder and how it could not have been Hunter as he was back at the bakery.

'Well did anyone see Mr. Hunter when he came back?'

'That is the problem dear. No one saw him, and he has no proof of his trip back to the bakery.' Susie said. Her hopes mounting that Patty would be willing to help them.

'Oh aye, so you have come to check my CCTV footage to see if we can spot Mr. Hunter entering the bakery at around that time then?'

'Yes,' both Meg and Susie said together with an optimistic tone.

'Can't help you sorry!'

Meg and Susie were taken aback. She had seemed so willing to hear them out, and they were both sure she would be willing to help save Hunter.

'Oh?' Susie said dumbfounded.

'Patty we would be ever grateful if you could assist us just to look.' Meg pleaded.

Patty wiped the bar with a wet old rag and then flung it over her shoulder. Her whole life had been spent smelling like moped up ale. She leaned forward with both hands on the bar.

'Just between you and me,' she said with a secretive look left and right, 'the CCTV cameras have never worked.'

'Oh no,' Meg said, her heart sinking.

'My old dad, May God rest his soul, installed the cameras he got from some junk shop years ago. And he tinkered with trying to get them to work, but he never did.'

'Oh, I see.' Susie's mind was already moving forward. Surely there must be other CCTV cameras in the street then. Her face had the look of a woman planning her next move.

'I can see what you're thinking Lady Carter. And you would be quite right to think so.'

'What's that?'

'The only place with working CCTV cameras though is the old art gallery on the corner. They would have a clear line of sight and no doubt actual footage.'

Meg and Susie thanked Patty for her help and for the tip about the art gallery cameras. Patty assured them it was more than alright, and they should drop in for lunch one day.

Heading to the door to go to the art gallery Patty called out after them.

'Will we have the pleasure of your company for the Pirates and Wenches Ball then Lady Carter?'

'She surely won't be a Pirate then.' joked Eddie Saunders, a local fisherman who spent long days at sea.

Raucous laughter filled the pub as they all thought about Lady Susie Carter dressed as a wench.

'Indeed, you will.' Susie replied joining in the spirit of the moment. 'And I may already have my wenches outfit.'

She smiled and together with Meg left the Smugglers Inn to a round of applause. The locals enjoyed a bit of banter and someone who could take a joke. Susie had won them over with her wenches' outfit line.

After making inquiries at the old art gallery, they left disappointed. The CCTV camera had malfunctioned. It might have picked up Hunter entering and leaving the bakery, but for the malfunction. The receptionsit had suggested there was a faulty wire.

Meg and Susie felt deflated as they returned to the car for the drive back to the castle. It seems their best chance of helping prove Hunter innocent had gone out the window.

As they left the Art Gallery, they passed the Council Chambers.

'Let's quickly drop in and say hello to Councilor Bradshaw.'

Bradshaw's office was small and dark. The blinds looked as though they had never been drawn open since the day they were installed. Thick layers of dust piled high not wanting to be disturbed.

Susie stood in the doorway sorry she had missed him.

She took a moment to survey his office. Councilor Bradshaw was a collector of local history memorabilia. The bookshelves were full of historical books recounting stories of struggle and victory.

Piled on top of one book shelve was a self-penned book titled 'Polmerton: The Last Three Hundred Years.'

'Oh, how clever of Bradshaw to have written a book and get it published.' She doubted it had a wide readership, yet she was certain it contained some fascinating stories of Polmerton.

With Meg waiting in the car she had to be quick. She had intended just to pop in and schedule a meeting for when she had more time. She jotted down a note to ask him to call when he had a free moment.

Returning the pen to its holder, she glanced momentarily at the old black and white photos lining the walls of his office.

'Oh, my,' she whispered to herself. One of them was a picture of Charles Ash III playing croquet on the lawns in front of Ash Castle. He was young and handsome. Probably taken before I was even born she thought to herself.

Below the photos, in a waste bin, she noticed rolled up plans.

'A quick look won't hurt.' She thought.

She pulled one out of the bin and unfolded it.

It was clearly a plan for a historic old building, and quite a significant one at that. But could it be Ash Castle she pondered?

'Can I help you?' A rather gruff voice from a stern looking, frumpy lady, asked. She had a look about her that suggested she was not to be messed with.

Susie dropped the plans embarrassed. 'Oh, I was just looking for Councilor Bradshaw.'

'Well, he's not here. Gone to some historical meeting in Penzance or some such.' She stated with annoyance. 'And who should I say called for him?'

'Oh, it's fine. I have left a note for him.'

'Right. Well, best you get on then.'

Susie took the hint. She thanked the frumpy looking lady and headed back out to the car to the waiting Meg. They pointed the car to home as Susie updated Meg on how it went.

She sounded disappointed Meg thought. 'Oh, I am sure he will call when he is in then.'

Woolsworth had left a note for Susie on the Kitchen table. It was an urgent message to call Aimee at the bakery.

'Good heavens. What on earth could it be?' Susie said out loud to no one in particular.

The note indicated that she had called on more than one occasion trying to get a hold of Susie. Susie grabbed the phone and called the number on the note.

'The Famous Polmerton Bakery?' she answered.

'Oh, hello dear, it's Susie Carter returning your call?'

'Oh, just one minute please.'

She had put the phone down to serve a customer. With Hunter gone she was finding she was run off her feet. Susie listened in as she finished serving the customer when another arrived. It seems like everyone in Polmerton had the afternoon munchies Susie thought to herself. A few minutes passed before she got back to the phone.

'Sorry Lady Carter, busy afternoon.'

'That's quite alright dear. Now how can I help?'

'Well, I had a thought. And I'm not sure if it will amount too much.'

'Go on?'

'Well, when Hunter returned to the bakery to get those yummy Strawberry Jam Tarts he is famous for, well I think I can prove he was actually at the bakery at the time of the murder!'

Susie's heart sped up. Is this the breakthrough she had hoped for? She wondered.

'You don't say?'

'Well, I am not sure if this helps or not, but when Hunter was back at the bakery, oh wait a minute ...'

She put the phone down again to serve more customers. From the sound of it, the new customers were the rather loud sounding American family Susie had seen earlier at the Smugglers Inn having lunch.

A few more minutes went by as Susie hung on waiting patiently.

'Back, so sorry. Now, where was I?'

'You were saying when Hunter was back at the bakery?'

'Oh yes, when he was here he sent me a message to say he was on his way back with the Strawberry Jam Tarts. He had left me in charge of the food at the party you see.'

'What sort of message did he send?'

'How do you mean sorry?'

'The message, you said he sent you a message?'

'Oh, right yes. He sent me a text message. I still have it on my phone.'

She put the phone down and went for her mobile phone. A few seconds later she was back to read out the message.

'He messaged me to say, Hope all is okay. I have the tart's and heading back now!'

'What time was it sent dear?'

'At exactly 8:20 pm.'

Susie's heart rate went even higher. If this were true, then Hunter would have an alibi.

'Terrific dear, now do me a favor. We will need your phone and that message as evidence. So, put it somewhere safe for the moment okay?'

'Of course,' she replied, her voice ringing with delight that she had helped in the investigation.

On hanging up the phone, Susie immediately called Inspector Reynolds to inform him of the breakthrough in the case. They discussed the matter briefly before he shattered her hopes.

The Inspector had suggested to her that, the fact he sent a text message meant nothing about his location at the time. He could have sent that message while standing over his victim's body. He concluded that while it was an interesting development, it looked more like a guilty man trying to manufacture an alibi.

Not being a technical person Susie had no grounds to argue the point with him. She assumed that he must know what he was talking about in such matters and resigned herself to the fact that this was not the breakthrough she had hoped for.

Hanging up the phone from the Inspector she felt somewhat deflated.

'Max! Where are you Max?' she called out. He always made her feel better.

Max came skidding around the corner. The shiny tiled floor in the kitchen was making quite the obstacle for him to change direction when he had momentum. His excitement bubbling over as he knew that tone of voice could only mean one thing.

A short time later a delighted Max was leading Susie up a winding track in the forest. The more they walked, the better she felt. Max, of course, was overcome with joy at spending time with his Master outdoors.

11

The next day Susie took a drive out to Carnon Downs.

It was good to have a change of scenery and explore some of the countrysides charms. It didn't take her more than a few minutes to find the Ocean View Home. It was a grand old Victorian building high on a hill. No doubt there was a glimpse of an ocean view somewhere. Susie doubted any of the residents might have retained sufficient vision to see it though.

She arrived at the reception area and asked to speak with Pamela Lawson.

A short time later she was seated in the lounge on a rather comfy couch having morning tea with Pamela.

They discussed the death of her daughter. The authorities had informed her that her darling Abigail had passed away.

'She was such a sweet girl, always very bright.'

'Sadly, I didn't get a chance to know her that well.'

'Oh, she was very fond of you Lady Carter'

'She was?'

'Oh yes, she always talked about you in high regard. Every time she visited me for years, she would talk about you.'

Susie wondered how that was possible but put it down to her losing her mind as one does when they get older.

'I used to love my visits to Ash Castle.'

'Oh, how often would you visit?'

'Well, Charles and I were very close you know. So, I came as often as I could. He usually sent a car to come and collect me.'

'Really?'

'Oh yes. Several times a week he would send his driver for me. Of course, he had his driver pick up me down at a quiet park so that no one saw, you know.'

'He did?' Susie was devouring a sponge cake with her tea and was fascinated by what she heard.

'We had a wonderful time together. It was like we were meant for each other but sadly could never truly be together. But the parties we had. Oh, they were so wonderful, just the three of us.'

'The three of you?'

'Oh yes, Charles and I, and of course Woolsworth would always join in. Such fun we had.'

Susie's mind was going wild with possibility. Surely, she wasn't saying what Susie thought she was saying; the three of them having parties together. Susie couldn't stand the thought of it all. She decided it was best to change the subject despite secretly desiring to know more.

'I was wondering, this whole business with poor Abigail, can you think of anyone who might have wanted to do her harm at all?'

'Well, I imagine there were a lot of people who didn't like her. She was a hard woman you know, but she had to be, as the Mayor.' She said sipping her tea and pondering the question.

'Quite right, not an easy job at all.'

'She was the captain of the ship of Polmerton. The crew don't always get along with the captain or agree with every decision.'

'Well, that's very true indeed. Did she have any problems with any of the crew do you know?'

'Oh no. Not that I am aware of. As far as I knew they all loved her.'

Susie was growing confused by the conversation. One minute she was saying that lots of people might have wanted to do her harm and the next everyone loved her. Perhaps the poor woman is losing her mind Susie concluded.

They chatted on for a bit about the weather and if it might rain or not.

Susie glanced at her watch and decided it was time to head back home. She was in the process of leaving when a thought popped into her mind.

'Pamela do you mind if I ask dear,' she asked delicately 'There is a giant portrait of Charles in the stairwell at Ash Castle. Do you remember it?'

'Oh yes, it's my favorite. I was there when he sat for it, on three occasions. It's a wonderful likeness.'

'Yes, it is. The other night when Abigail came to the party, I couldn't help but notice that her side profile in the right light, was remarkably like the portrait of Charles?'

Susie decided just to put the question out there and see what sort of response she got. She wasn't entirely sure how to ask directly if the poor woman was having an affair with Charles.

'Oh, they do look alike don't they?' she marveled at the memories.

'Well, there is a remarkable likeness, yes.'

'She was so fond of her father.'

'Who? Abigail?'

'Yes of course. She loved Charles madly even though he never recognized her as his own.'

'Oh, I see.'

'Yes. Charles is going to leave Ash Castle to her when he passes on. She does love that old castle you know.'

'Well, I imagine so.'

Susie thanked her for her time and headed out to her much-loved Land Rover for the drive back to Polmerton. The whole way back all she could think about was the fact that Mayor Abigail McGill was the illegitimate child of Charles Ash III. And what's more, she was under the impression she was going to inherit his estate.

Of course, the poor woman did appear to be losing her mind, so how much of what she had to say could be taken as gospel Susie wondered.

Woolsworth greeted Susie at the door when she arrived back.

'Greetings Ma'am. May I inquire as to what time you will be taking tea this afternoon? One has a lot of dusting to do today, and I want to schedule my time?'

'Oh yes, well I might skip tea this afternoon Woolsworth, thank you.'

'Very good Ma'am.'

'Tell me something Woolsworth. Do you know Pamela Lawson?'

'Yes Ma'am, from some time ago. I believe she has lost her mind in some home somewhere.'

'How did you know her?'

'She would visit from time to time.'

Max came scooting down the stairs at the sound of Susie's voice. He had built up momentum as he hit the tiled floors in the foyer and skidded across the floor and slammed into Woolworth's leg.

Woolsworth screamed at the wretched beast and departed the scene. Susie wondered if he had made his exit so hastily to avoid any further questions about Pamela Lawson.

'Max, how are you, darling boy?' Susie asked as she rubbed the back of his head. He was as excited as ever to see her. She marveled at how he could generate the same level of enthusiasm for seeing her each day.

Max looked up at her with his adorable brown eyes and smiled. His tongue hanging from the side of his mouth, and his tail working overtime.

'Now, we must go and speak with young Meg.'

On hearing her name, Max led the way through the maze of hallways and corridors to the office where Meg was busy at the computer. She was such a diligent worker Susie had thought.

'Hello Susie, how was your road trip?'

'It was very enlightening indeed.'

For the moment she decided to keep the possibility that Abigail McGill was the illegitimate child of Charles Ash III to herself. If she was, then she may have had rights to the estate. But at this stage, it was the word of an old woman who was clearly losing her mind with age. Never the less, there was a remarkable likeness between Abigail and Charles. She decided she needed to get to the bottom of this.

'How are you getting on?' Susie asked Meg.

'Very well, in fact, I have been doing some research as you asked.'

'What about dear?'

'Jess Muller.'

'Oh, go on, what have you found out?'

'Well, it seems that Jess Muller may not be the most reliable witness after all.'

Meg pulled up an archived news article from seven years ago in the Exeter Express and Echo. The article was about the trial of a rogue accountant who had made off with the trust account stealing his client's money. Jess, who had worked for the accountant at the time, was giving testimony in his defense.

The judge had thrown out her testimony as inadmissible due to the highly exaggerated nature. She was dismissed, and her former boss eventually was sentenced to a ten-year term in prison.

'Oh, that is good work Meg. When we present this to the Inspector, he will realize that she is hardly a solid witness to build a case around.'

'Exactly right, and it gets even better.' Meg said pleased with herself.

'How is that then?'

'She liked to cry wolf.'

Meg pulled up the second article also from the Exeter Express and Echo. The article was titled 'Rape Victim Says She Lied.'

Susie read the article in a bit of shock. It seems a then-teenage Jess Muller had accused a former boyfriend of raping her. When the matter started getting serious with police investigations, she withdrew the allegation saying she was just seeking attention. At the time the police gave her a serious talking to and a warning.

'Wonderful news,' Susie exclaimed praising Meg 'this might be all we need to get Hunter released. Without their star witness, the Inspector will not have a leg to stand on to keep Hunter locked up.'

Meg's face was all smiles. She loved to be able to do something positive, and she enjoyed working with Susie. They made a great team she thought.

'You have a real talent for research Meg.'

'Well, I do enjoy playing the sleuth with you.'

'Now, what do you know about mobile phones?'

Susie explained to her that Hunter had sent a text message from the bakery to his assistant Amiee at approximately the time of the murder.

She asked if Meg knew of or could find out if a text message could be traced to the location it was sent from and too. Unsure of the answer Meg jumped back on Google to do the necessary research.

Five minutes later a happy Meg informed Susie that a text message could indeed be traced based on which mobile cells the message originated from and went too.

Susie thanked her and went to phone Inspector Reynolds.

'Reynolds here?'

'Inspector Reynolds I have some news I think you will find very interesting.'

She explained the background information they had on Jess Muller, and why she would not stand up in court as a reliable witness. After concluding her news, she demanded that the Inspector release Hunter from the lock up immediately.

'I'm afraid that won't be possible Ma'am.'

'And why is that then?' she demanded.

'Because I am afraid that Mr. McGill is no longer here!'

Susie was shocked. For a moment she couldn't speak.

'Well, where on earth is he then?'

'He's been rushed to Plymouth Hospital earlier today.'

12

Hunter sat up in his hospital bed when Susie arrived. Relief flooded through her when she realized he was okay. In fact, he appeared to be more than okay relishing all the attention from the nurses.

The room overflowed with flowers and cards from well-wishers. One thing that can be said about the people of Polmerton is they are quick to react when one of their own is in a spot of bother. Susie reasoned that it was to do with the fishing village culture. If a fishing boat got into trouble on rough seas, the entire village would rally together to get them home safely. For that reason, the emergency rescue boat was always at the ready at the top of the slipstream.

They embraced with a gentle hug. Susie gave him a peck on his forehead relieved that he was in good shape.

'What on earth happened?'

'Well, I am not sure really. One minute I was watching TV in my cell. I had just had dinner that the Constable had brought in for me. The next thing I know I wake up here with doctors and nurses poking and fussing about me.'

'Oh, good heavens.'

'You can say that again. It seems the old ticker had a turn for the worse.'

Susie checked the charts at the end of the bed. Nothing about a heart attack or stroke on it. A bad case of indigestion it appeared.

'We are going to have to get you into better shape, so, you look after yourself,' she said with a smile and poked him in the tummy.

'Oh, right yes.'

'And I hear you have some good news?'

'Indeed, I do. It appears the Inspector has released me.'

'You don't say?'

'Something about some GPS co-ordinates proving I was at the bakery at the time of the murder so it couldn't have been me.'

'Oh, you don't say?' Susie smiled to herself.

'Yes, good to see the Inspector did some actual police work then.' He laughed.

'Now that might be pushing it a bit far.' She joined him in laughter, and the two of them laughed for the next few minutes, more from relief than anything.

For the next hour, they joked and chatted like long lost friends. Talk soon turned to the cooking school and the plans they needed to make. The first-weekend class was scheduled for just six weeks away. So, there was a lot that needed to be done.

Susie grabbed a notepad and pen and made notes. An action list of things for them both to do was created. It was agreed they would enlist the help of Meg who had proved herself to be an excellent worker, and highly skilled in administration and events work.

Hunter excused himself for a moment as he visited the bathroom.

Curious Susie started to look at all the get well soon cards. She picked up each one in turn and read the message from each well-wisher. The last of them was one from Laura Hamilton. It simply read 'Get Well Soon Hunter! We Need You :)'.

Unsure what the meaning behind "we need you" was, she placed the card back down as Hunter re-entered the room. There was something about the card though that had her intrigued. She just couldn't place what it was.

Hunter and Susie talked some more developing their plans for the cooking school. Some discussion developed around the idea of having to go on a study trip to the French Riviera to research how other cooking schools are run. Sounded like a fun little getaway they both agreed though Susie wondered if Hunter's motives might have been more than just food. Still, she didn't mind the attention at all.

After several hours the nurse informed Susie that it was time the patient got some more rest so that he could be sent home tomorrow. Susie stood up and accidentally knocked the cards on the floor.

She bent over and scooped them all up. As she picked them up, it struck her, the handwriting from Laura Hamilton. That is what had intrigued her earlier. She just couldn't place it at the time. She was sure she had seen it somewhere before, but where?

As Susie drove back to Polmerton, she couldn't get the thought out of her mind. She had seen the handwriting on the card from Laura Hamilton before, but where?

It was driving her crazy. She was so preoccupied with the thought she was having trouble navigating the narrow winding roads on the approach into town. A Lorrie swerved to avoid her and clipped some trees in the process. She didn't even notice.

As she rounded a sweeping bend which offered some of the best views across Polmerton, save for Ash Castle, the thought flashed in her mind.

'I've got it!' she cried out.

Satisfied now that she had the answer she sped on into town.

Ten minutes later she burst into the police station alarming the Inspector and the Constable. She hadn't time for pleasantries. It was obvious to them she meant business.

'Didn't expect to see you back now that Hunter is no longer our number one suspect?' Inspector Reynolds asked.

'Inspector, you had previously shown me a letter from my great uncle's bedside table.'

'Oh aye, yes.'

'May I look at it please?'

Inspector Reynolds fussed about looking for the file on Charles Ash III's death. He walked out into the back office where the cases getting less attention were piled high on top of each other.

A moment later he was back with the file. He held the letter out to Susie.

'This one then?'

'Oh yes, that is the one.'

Susie studied the letter through her reading glasses. The letter clearly indicated that the writer of the letter knew something about Charles Ash III that would be revealed if he didn't pay an amount of two hundred and fifty thousand pounds.

'And what is all this about then?'

'Well, I was visiting with Hunter in the hospital. He had a lovely collection of 'get well soon' cards. But one of them ...'

'One of them was a match for the handwriting on this blackmail note then?'

'Yes, quite right.'

'You're becoming quite the investigator then Lady Carter' Inspector Reynolds joked. 'And whose handwriting do you believe it belonged to?'

'Well, one card from Laura Hamilton is very similar to this, though I cannot be sure if it is an exact match or not.'

Susie was less certain now than she was earlier that this was a match. Still, it was worth following through, as a possible lead on what might have happened to Charles Ash.

'We can have forensics run some tests and compare the two. If it's a match, they will soon be able to tell.'

Inspector Reynolds opened his filing cabinet and pulled out an order form to send off to forensics. He entered all the details of what he wanted them to check as far as the handwriting analysis was concerned.

'And what do you think Ms. Hamilton's motive might have been for blackmailing old man Ash then?'

'Well, money I guess.'

Susie paused a moment. She hadn't really thought much about a motive at all.

'I tell you one thing then. She had more of a motive to kill the Mayor than your old uncle.'

'Because of the affair with her husband?'

'Yes that.' the Inspector stroked his chin thinking, 'and the fact that the Mayor cost the Hamilton's a lot of money. Possibly into the millions'

'I'm not sure I follow.'

'Well, the Hamilton's were in partnership with Mr. Heath Henshaw for that property development. The one the Mayor blocked.'

'So, she was the only obstacle preventing them from making millions.' Susie pondered the possibility. It was obvious that Laura Hamilton was still distraught with the Mayor for sleeping with her husband. That much was clear. So clear that her grievances were out on display at the opening night party.

'Yes indeed. There were a few frustrated folks with her then.'

'She was very drunk on the night of my party.'

'Yes, from what I hear she was well drunk.'

'But she couldn't have been involved with the murder of the Mayor. Her husband had taken her home in the middle of the Mayoral speech and put her to bed.' Susie informed the Inspector.

They talked on about the fact that Laura Hamilton could have slipped back to the party. She was after all just next door as the crow flies. It would not have been at all difficult for her to come through a servant's quarters in the rear of the castle to find Abigail. After whacking her on the head, she could have slipped back out and home to bed.

Inspector Reynolds decided to pursue this new possibility. With their star witness no longer credible, and their number one suspect clearly innocent, they didn't have anything else to go on.

Susie bid them farewell.

She decided to return to the hospital and get a copy of the card Laura Hamilton had sent him. The Inspector had been kind enough to give her a copy of the blackmail note for her records.

Back home she called for Woolsworth.

He was up a small ladder with a flowery apron around his waist. His arm extended with a feather duster attached dusting the tops of the window sills.

'Woolsworth I wonder if I might have a word.'

He looked down from his fragile position and cursed her under his breath. At his age, it had taken a good while, and considerable risk, to get up the damned steps. Now she wanted him down. He muttered his discontent away as he gingerly descended the four steps to the floor.

'Yes, Ma'am? Is it afternoon tea you require?'

'Oh, that would be delightful yes.'

'Certainly.' he said as he turned to head to the Kitchen.

'Wait, that's not what I wanted to chat with you about.'

'Ma'am?'

Susie asked Woolsworth, who knew every nook and cranny of the old castle better than anyone alive, if it was possible for someone to come in through the servant's quarters at the back and make their way to the pool room undetected.

Woolsworth came alive with the idea.

His fondest childhood memories were of playing hide and seek in the various corridors and passages with young Charlie. The two of them would spend hours he recounted finding the best hiding places, secret passages between rooms that few people knew about.

Susie listened with fascination. She could imagine a young Woolsworth, the son of the Butler, and young Charles Ash III son of Charles Ash II playing together when they were young.

Woolsworth led Susie out to the rear of the castle to where the servant's quarters were. These days they were just used for storage and the like. He showed her several entries in and out of the back of the castle that anyone with the knowledge of them could easily access.

Susie followed Woolsworth as he opened a door leading into a secret passage between the servant's quarters and a small hallway at the rear of the dining room. The passage was dark and musty smelling. Cobwebs lined the walls undisturbed for years until just recently.

'I believe this could have made an excellent escape route for the culprit.' Woolsworth summed up after giving his tour.

'How many people would know about this secret passage then?'

'Not many I suspect.' Woolsworth said. In his mind, he thought that possibly he was the only one who knew about them, but he didn't dare say so.

Susie pondered the possibility that the Mayor's killer could have slipped into the servant's quarters while the party was in full swing. They could have then found the secret passage and arrived in the pool room where they lay in wait for the Mayor. Then using the same route could have slipped out of the pool room just in time before Hunter McGill entered the room.

She ran the whole plan by Woolsworth for his reaction.

'Sounds plausible Ma'am.'

She nodded thinking it was more than just plausible. She was going to call the Inspector to get him to take a closer look to see if they could piece together a more accurate picture of what had taken place.

'Yes indeed. Woolsworth, a question for you.'

'Ma'am?'

'Were you aware that someone was trying to blackmail Charles for the sum of two hundred and fifty thousand pounds?'

'No Ma'am.' Woolsworth replied, his face not registering any surprise or shock.

'Would you have any idea why someone would do so?'

'No Ma'am. I didn't mess in his affairs'

Woolsworth departed to go and make afternoon tea.

Susie went to find Meg. She wanted her to go back through all the accounts to see if any large sums of money had been paid out by Charles to anyone in the last few years.

13

Susie had just finished up dinner and had settled into the lounge by an open fire. She loved a good book and was fortunate to find an Agatha Christie mystery in the library bookshelves.

Barely making it through page one, Woolsworth appeared in the doorway.

'Ma'am you have a visitor. Are you free?'

'Who on earth is it at this hour?'

'It's your neighbor Mr. Douglas Hamilton'

'Oh, heavens,' Susie was unprepared for visitors but assumed it must be important for him to arrive at this hour unannounced. She instructed Woolsworth to show him into the lounge room.

Douglas Hamilton arrived in the lounge and exchanged greetings with Susie. She poured him a tawny port, and they sat down together on the couch.

'To what do I owe the pleasure then Mr. Hamilton?'

'Oh, I insist you call me Dougy. All my close friends do.' He smiled at her oozing with charm.

'I imagine they do.' Susie smiled back.

'Well, I saw your light on and thought I would pop in to see how you were getting settled.'

Susie thought about the question of getting settled for a moment. It seemed like a lifetime since she had made the move from York to start a new life in Ash Castle. Overall, she felt she had settled in very nicely despite the tragic events on the night of the party.

After a quarter of an hour of small talk, Douglas Hamilton decided it was now or never. He couldn't imagine a better time to bring it up.

'Susie, I wonder if I could ask you a question. Something of a personal matter if that is alright?'

'I'm sure it will be fine?'

'Thank you. Well as it turns out Charles, and I were in the middle of a rather large property transaction at the time of his unfortunate passing.'

'Is that right?'

'Yes, it seems that he was in a spot of bother financially, and I had offered to help him out by buying some land he had no use for you see.'

'Very good of you to offer,' Susie smiled. Inside, though, she thought that the only reason he would offer to help would be if there were a profit to be made somewhere along the line.

'Well, I like to help where I can.'

'And what were your plans for the land Mr. Hamilton?'

'Well, none really. I had no real use for the land at all. Just that it backed onto my land, so it would have made a nice little addition, you know.'

Susie was sure there was more to it than just a gesture of kindness towards her uncle. A thought flashed through her mind. When she was at the office of Henshaw Property Developments, she was sure she saw plans on the wall for townhouses high on the hill behind the castle to capture the view. She made a mental note to check it out.

'I see.'

'Yes, well, the transaction was set to take place, but he passed away. Rather unfortunate.'

'Yes, bad timing it seems.'

'Quite right yes. I was wondering if now might be an opportune time for us to conclude this business. I have all the paperwork with me.'

With that, Douglas Hamilton reached into the inside pocket of his tweed jacket and pulled out a contract and placed it before Susie. He placed a pen on the table ready for her to sign the paperwork.

Susie sat back in her chair and took a sip of her tawny port considering her words carefully.

'Mr. Hamilton, whatever business you had agreed with Charles is no longer relevant as he has passed on.'

'Well, I do believe it is relevant. The deal was already agreed to. It was just a matter of settlement which couldn't take place at the time. I feel you have an obligation to follow through with Charles wishes.'

'Mr. Hamilton, I didn't know Charles that well. However, I am certain his highest intention would have been to preserve Ash Castle at all costs including the surrounding estate.'

Douglas Hamilton was starting to become a touch frustrated. Old man Ash had been hard enough work to get him to agree to sell the land. Now this newcomer was proving more difficult than he had imagined.

'Well yes, but, the estate lost a lot of money and cost's a small fortune to run. If I buy the land from you for a good price, then it will save you a spot of bother I dare say.'

'Perhaps that was a workable solution for my uncle. However, with the start of the cooking school in a few weeks, I think we can manage just fine.'

'I see.' Douglas decided that he was not going to progress his cause any further with this approach. New tactics would be needed he decided. He took a sip of his tawny port.

They continued with some polite small talk, Douglas sharing with her a little about the upcoming Pirates & Wenches Convention and what fun it was. He joked with her that he was going to put her name down for a part in the annual Pirates & Wenches Musical performed at the Smugglers Inn.

'Well I think it might be time that I bid you good evening then,' Douglas eventually said standing up. Susie stood with him and shook his hand to conclude the conversation. They walked across the lounge room and into the foyer to the front door.

'How is your lovely wife Laura?' Susie asked standing with the front door open ready for Douglas to depart.

'Oh, well she has recovered from her turn the other night. But she is a bit shaken up I am afraid.'

'Oh, how so?'

'Well, it seems the police were around at our place earlier making inquiries. With Hunter McGill in the clear, they are looking for the next most likely suspect. It seems Laura might be it.'

'Oh, good heavens!' Susie faked her surprise at the news.

'Yes, but, it's clear as day that she couldn't have been involved.'

'It is?'

'Well yes of course. She was in bed at the time of the murder. I put her there myself.'

'I see. And did you return to the party after that?'

'Oh yes of course. Love a good party. Well good evening Susie.'

'So long Mr. Hamilton.'

After seeing Douglas Hamilton out the door, Susie went to the kitchen to make herself a hot chocolate. She found it helped her sleep straight through the night, though she wasn't in the mood for sleep tonight.

Her mind was swirling around with the possibilities.

On the one hand, she was relieved that Hunter was now out of the Inspectors sights for murder. But it left the question of who the culprit might be. More importantly, the murderer was walking amongst the good people of Polmerton.

Could they strike again? She wondered.

She sipped on her hot chocolate with two marshmallows and went through each of the key suspects as she saw things. Of course, Laura Hamilton was shaping up as the next most likely.

And what of the handwritten note threatening Charles.

She wasn't at all sure what to make of it. Is it possible that Laura Hamilton was blackmailing Charles? And if so for what? Surely Charles wouldn't have paid up.

Lost in her thoughts, and totally enjoying the hot chocolate, she didn't hear it at first.

Max did, though. He had been sitting by her side when his ears detected the sounds of movement outside. He barked and ran to the front door.

Susie froze at first. She glanced at the clock and thought it was unusual for visitors at this hour. Woolsworth had long since gone to bed, and Meg was out late on a date with Constable Daniels finally.

She cautiously followed Max to the front door. Her heart sped up as she heard footsteps on the landing.

'Who is it?' she cried out trying to mask the fear in her voice.

The door handle turned. Max barked. Susie gasped in fear.

'Oh, it's just me Susie.'

Douglas Hamilton had returned and let himself in and was now standing in the entrance hall. The look in his eyes was a man filled with both rage and determination.

Susie glanced around for something to protect herself with. This was most unexpected, and she wasn't sure what he might be capable of. On seeing a familiar face, Max stopped his barking and sat by Susie's side.

'Oh, Mr. Hamilton you startled me.'

'Sorry about that.'

'How can I help you? It's getting late you know?'

Douglas walked to the grand staircase and took a seat on the third bottom step. He sighed as he rested his elbows on his knees and put his head in his hands. He looked like a defeated man on the verge of a breakdown.

Susie said nothing, waiting for him to explain himself.

'Yes, I am sorry to return and give you a fright.' He said his words barely audible. 'But I just couldn't leave without putting up a fight!'

'A fight?'

'Well yes. It seems like the coppers have it in for Laura, trying to get her to confess to the murder of that stupid woman.'

'So, you don't believe it was Laura then?' Susie asked cautiously.

Douglas laughed at the suggestion.

'Unlikely,' he said through belly laughs. 'She wouldn't harm a soul, really. She talks with a lot of spite at times, but when it's all said and done, she is totally harmless.'

'Well, you have nothing to worry about then?'

Susie was going through a range of options on how to get him back out the front door. He seemed unstable emotionally, and she feared for her life. Clearly, he was troubled by something.

'Whether she did it or not is hardly the point is it?' he glared at her.

'Well if she is innocent, then she has nothing to answer for.'

'No. But even if she didn't do it, there are folks around these parts who will still try to lock her up for it. That's just the way things are.'

Douglas Hamilton stood up. Anguish filled his face. He adored Laura and would do anything to protect her. Sure, they had their ups and downs. Sure, he had been caught on more than one occasion having extramarital affairs. But he adored and loved her, anyway. And he would stop at nothing to protect her.

'I'm not sure I follow.'

Susie was backing up slowly trying not to show any signs of fear. Hamilton had gone from being rather charming earlier on, to now intimidating. She was preparing to make a break for the kitchen where she could lock herself in and call the police.

'All I am trying to say is, I don't think Laura has it in her to be a killer.'

'I see.'

'And we shouldn't assume her guilt without any evidence!'

His voice rose, and his face had become red with tension. It was as if he was in some sort of trance. He had taken several steps towards her and was at an arm's length.

Susie decided to make a break for it the second his eyes diverted from hers.

'Anyway, I've overstayed my welcome,' he said snapping out of the menacing state he was in. 'I must be off, or Laura will be mad.'

With that, he turned on his heels and went back out through the front door.

Her heart pounding in her chest Susie ran to the front door and closed it tight. She peeked out the peephole to watch Douglas Hamilton walk across the car park.

Relieved she patted Max and caught her breath.

'What was all that about?' she asked Max and patted his head.

Slowly her heart rate returned to normal, and she decided she needed to get some rest. Time for bed and read a few pages of a good book. That should get her to sleep.

She walked down the hallway towards the kitchen.

That's when she saw the gun pointed at her.

14

Susie screamed at the sight of the gun pointed at her chest. It was the last thing she had expected. Coming out of the dark the intruders face moved into the light. Susie was shocked to see her though not surprised.

And it was clear she had been drinking heavily.

The stench of alcohol filled Susie's nostrils as the woman screamed at her.

'Where is he?' her face full of rage.

'He's not here dear.' Susie said trying to remain calm. 'Now just calm down and we can talk about things.'

'There is nothing left to talk about.'

Susie was backing slowly up the hallway towards the entry hall. The woman followed each step still menacing Susie with the gun.

'Now, what seems to be the problem?'

'You know what the problem is!' she screamed back at Susie. 'You've been sleeping with my Dougy!'

Susie was horrified at the suggestion. It was the furthest thing from her mind, and she was sure the furthest thing from Douglas Hamilton's mind as well.

'What on earth makes you think that Laura?'

Laura Hamilton was in a rage. She had been drinking since the police came to chat with her about the murder of Abigail McGill.

They had made it clear that she was their number one suspect now that the baker was off the hook.

She had tried to explain to the Inspector that she couldn't have done it as she was home in bed having made a scene at the party. The Inspector explained to her that the scene she made, and her obvious displeasure with the Mayor for sleeping with her husband, gave her the strongest of motives.

The Inspector had informed her that it would have been easy for her to slip back to the party, do the Mayor in, and then slip back home undetected.

Laura was outraged at the idea. The fact is that she had a perfect alibi. She was just too embarrassed to tell the Inspector. So, she said nothing.

When the police departed, Laura started drinking. And not drinking just any old thing. She went into Douglas's den and found his twenty-year-old whiskey Glen Dronach that he kept for special occasions. This was one she reasoned.

Halfway through the bottle she looked out her bedroom window towards the castle and saw her Dougy entering through the front door. A good hour or so had passed, and he still hadn't returned. That could only mean one thing she thought. She had finally had it with all his sleeping around. And now he was sleeping with the old bat in the castle. Enough was enough.

'I saw him come in here. And he hasn't come home yet!' Laura said waving the gun around.

It was clear to Susie that Laura Hamilton was so drunk she might fall at any moment. She just needed to stay calm until her opportunity arrived. Of course, the fear that, in her drunken state she might do something silly was also very real.

'Yes, he was here Laura, but it's not what you are thinking.' Susie said trying to reason with her.

'Of course, it was!'

'What makes you think so?'

'Because he always sleeps around on me!' she screamed.

'He was just paying a visit to chat.'

'Do you think I'm a fool?' Laura yelled at Susie and raised the gun to her head. The gun was inches away from Susie's head. Her heart raced out of control. She was in a state of shock and shaking yet fighting to remain calm.

Laura motioned with the gun for Susie to walk in the direction of the lounge. So, drunk she could barely stand up Laura frantically waved the gun at Susie indicating she meant business. She told Susie to move in a drunken slur.

'Dear, I know you have been under a lot of stress lately,' Susie said in a calming voice despite the terror she felt. 'But I think we should put the gun down and talk.'

Laura laughed the laugh of a drunk confronting their own reflection in a mirror.

Frustrated by Susie not moving fast enough she gave Susie a shove in the back to hurry her along. It took Susie by surprise sending her forward in a lurching motion. She seized on the opportunity and made sure she bumped into the small side table positioned at the entrance to the lounge. The table held a blue china vase with freshly cut daisies.

Susie managed to bump the vase hard enough that it toppled off the edge of the small table and crashed into a hundred shredded and jagged pieces. It landed with a crashing sound that would have woken the heaviest sleeper.

She prayed that it had woken the one person who was able to help her.

Startled by the crash Laura shoved Susie again into the lounge room.

'Sit!' she demanded.

Susie did as she was told pleading with Laura to put the gun down.

Laura was so drunk she was struggling to stand and placed herself on the large glass coffee table that filled the void between the two elegant leather couches.

'How long have you been seeing my Dougy then?'

Susie was astonished at the question. In all her years, she had never been accused of such a thing, and under normal circumstances, she would have protested at the very nature of the question.

These were not ordinary circumstances though.

She tried to explain that she had no interest in Doug Hamilton.

'I'm sure that's what they all say. You know he used to love me once.' Laura said, her mind drifting off to a happier time.

'No doubt he still does dear.'

Laura became outraged at the suggestion. The hand holding the gun which had been languishing at her side came back to life. Susie stared down the muzzle of the gun, fearing the worse.

'If he loved me so damn much why was he sleeping with you and all the others?'

'Well I am not sure he was.'

'You have to die now like the rest!'

On hearing the crashing vase, Woolsworth stirred.

It sounded like the vase he treasured dearly. The blue china vase he liked to place the yellow daisies in. He treasured it as it was a gift from Charles. Charles, of course, knew precisely what to get his lover as the ideal gift.

Usually, Woolsworth would have slept through a bomb going off, but the sound of his favorite vase being smashed woke him instantly in the way a cry from a newborn wakes its mother.

Donning a dressing gown and slippers, he went out of the servant's quarters, through the kitchen and down the long hall to the entry foyer.

Muffled voices could be heard coming from the lounge.

As he got closer, it was clear there was some sort of commotion that had caused his vase to be smashed. Fragments of shattered clay crunching under his slipper as he took some nervous steps towards the doorway to the lounge.

There in the dim light, he saw what he thought was Laura Hamilton pointing a pistol at the head of Lady Carter in a menacing manner. He heard Laura threaten to kill her.

Thinking on his feet, he decided he needed to call the police. He turned to dash back to the kitchen where the phone hung on the wall and would be out of hearing range of the lounge.

As he took of Laura caught movement out of the corner of her eye. She turned to the door to see who or what it was.

Woolsworth heard her call out to see who was there. Then he heard Susie's voice reassuring her that it was probably just Max roaming around. Then more murmuring and the yelling of slurred instructions to Susie.

He scurried back to the Kitchen and called the Inspector who just happened to be in the office wrapping up some details of a petty theft case from earlier that day. The Inspector instructed him to try to calm the Hamilton woman down and try to distract her. Readily agreeing Woolsworth headed back to the lounge room.

'Evening Ma'am, will you require tea for your guest?' he said clearing his throat as he entered the room.

Startled, Laura Hamilton swung around to see who had just entered. She had forgotten that Woolsworth would be about somewhere. She waved the gun in his direction motioning for him to take a seat.

Woolsworth was quick to reply, 'Certainly Mrs. Hamilton, right after I make a pot of tea.' He went to turn and leave the lounge.

'Sit down you old fool!' she screamed at him.

He gingerly took a seat next to Susie thinking better of running afoul of the crazy drunk woman with the gun.

'You've been spying on us!'

'Not at all, Ma'am; I was asleep and awoke to find we had visitors. So, I came down to offer tea for you both.'

Laura was confused now. She wasn't sure where exactly to point the gun, so she waved it about between the two of them. She also wasn't sure what she was going to do next. If she shot the old bag, then she was going to have to shoot Woolsworth as well.

'Laura, why don't you put the gun down and let Woolsworth make us a nice pot of tea to enjoy. Then we can chat?'

Laura snapped.

It was the final straw for her.

All the stress and tension of her life came to a boiling point in this one moment in time.

'Shut up you old bag!' she screamed at Susie.

Laura jumped to her feet and pressed the gun to Susie's forehead.

'I've had it with you!' she screamed.

15

Constable Daniels and Meg had a lovely night.

It was their first date after being sweet on each other for a year or so since he first came to town. They enjoyed the night down at the Smugglers Inn where they shared the seafood platter.

Now standing on the steps of Ash Castle it was time to say good night.

Meg was desperately hoping that he might kiss her good night.

No doubt he wanted to, but clearly unsure how to go about it. A tense few moments of small talk and good nights as they both lingered.

Finally, Meg decided to take matters into her own hands. She reached up and kissed Constable Daniels gently on the lips. Somewhat surprised, yet excited, he kissed her back. With their lips locked together, they barely noticed the sound of the car pulling into the car park.

Inspector Reynolds had seen them kissing on the steps. Good for you lad he thought to himself. But there was a more pressing matter at hand. He closed the door of his car and cleared his throat.

'Alright, you two.'

Meg and Constable Daniels were startled. Lost in the moment, they didn't hear the car, and it was the last thing they were expecting. They certainly had no idea of the commotion inside.

Inspector Reynolds took them over to the cover of the old oak tree and explained the situation to them. Meg gasped with terror. She prayed nothing happened to Susie as she so loved having her around.

They discussed what they should do.

'We could go in through the servant's entry at the back. Then there is a walkway that leads to a small room just off the lounge. You wouldn't know it, but there is a doorway between the two large bookcases between the two rooms.'

'Oh aye,' said the Inspector listening and developing a plan. 'Here is what we will do then. Meg you come with me and show me the way into the small room. I can surprise her from there. Constable, you go in through the front door and make your way to the lounge.'

They all agreed on the plan.

Meg led the Inspector to the doorway around the back that once upon a time was the servant's entrance. It was also where the suppliers of produce would arrive each day.

Entering through the door, she found the passage that led to the small room next to the lounge. The Inspector had his standard issue pistol drawn at the ready.

The small room next to the lounge was a disused reading room. It would have offered some peace and quiet to those wanting to lose themselves in a good read back in the day. Today it was a storage room full of dusty old boxes.

There was a small peephole in the wall which gave a view between the books on the bookshelves in the lounge. From there the entire room could be clearly seen.

The Inspector took in the scene. Laura Hamilton was sitting on the coffee table with her back to the room he and Meg were in. This was good he thought as it gave them the element of surprise.

Hamilton had the gun raised and was yelling something at Susie. The gun appeared to be pointed at Susie's head. A terrified Woolsworth sat rocking back and forth next to Susie.

He also noticed with some relief that the young Constable had positioned himself just outside the lounge room door. He waited for the moment when he was needed to burst into action.

Whispering to Meg, he informed her to wait here until he and the Constable had the situation under control. She readily agreed though she was frightened that things might go horribly wrong.

And then Laura had stood up. Something had clearly agitated her. She was yelling at Susie.

She had the gun fixed clearly at her head.

The Inspector sensed the situation had escalated. Years of experience had taught him to read the signs. He decided now was the time to act.

He burst through the hidden door into the lounge with his gun firmly fixed on Laura Hamilton.

Laura, Susie and Woolsworth were not expecting the Inspector to appear in the lounge room suddenly. All three of them jumped at the same time.

'Alright, now Mrs. Hamilton; let's put the gun down.'

Unsure what to do Laura backed up so she could see both the Inspector and Susie. The gun swinging left and right not fixing on anyone. Her mind was swirling with confusion. She needed another drink badly.

'I'm going to kill her.' She said. 'She has been sleeping with my Dougy.'

Constable Daniels had entered the lounge through the main doors and made his way over to Woolsworth. He was going to try to get Woolsworth and Lady Carter out the door while the Inspector had Laura distracted.

'Now Mrs. Hamilton,' replied the Inspector. 'I am sure she has done no such thing.'

'She has, I saw him here with her.'

'He was just paying a visit dear.' Susie said still astonished at the accusation.

'It will be best for all concerned if you put the gun down now.'

Laura took a step towards the Inspector. Her gun now clearly pointing in his direction. His gun fixed on her. He was reminded of the tense standoffs in old westerns.

Constable Daniels had managed to slip out with Woolsworth to the relative safety of the Kitchen.

'And why is that then?' Laura asked the Inspector.

'That way no one gets hurt.' He reasoned with her. 'I know you don't want to hurt anyone Laura, but you need to put the gun down.'

'She has been having a filthy affair with my husband.' Laura explained swinging the gun in the direction of Susie, indicating who she thought the culprit was.

'Now I am sure it's all a misunderstanding Laura.'

She swung her attention back to the Inspector.

Susie tried to move herself along the rather large leather couch to the end where Woolsworth had been sitting. If the Inspector could distract her for long enough, she could make good her escape with the help of the young Constable.

'I saw them together.' Laura screamed at the top of her voice and turned back to where Susie had been sitting. When she noticed that Susie had moved, she became outraged and fixed the gun on her. Her finger which had been loosely hanging around the trigger now squeezed the trigger. Susie froze in her tracks.

Max sensing how severe the situation was, burst into the room and leaped into the air, his mouth wide open, he latched onto Laura Hamilton's wrist that held the gun.

His jaw locked hard breaking the bones in her wrist. His momentum and the grip he had on her wrist ensured that she fell backward. Max crashed down on top of her. The gun went flying across the room which Constable Daniels was quick to grab hold of.

Max wasn't letting up. He had sensed this woman was threatening his master and he would do anything to ensure she wasn't harmed. He held firm his grip as Laura cried out in pain.

Inspector Reynolds holstered his weapon and rushed over to handcuff Laura's free arm to the leg of the lounge chair.

It took a moment, but a shaken Susie was able to calm Max down. She reassured him that the danger had passed, and that he had done a good job. Meg entered the lounge and led Susie away to the kitchen were Woolsworth had poured a stiff brandy for them all.

With Laura in handcuffs and the gun clearly out of sight, everyone felt better. They all relaxed just a little.

Laura was either sobering up with the seriousness of the situation, or she had snapped out of the trance she was in. It was now dawning on her just how serious things were, and what she had done.

The Inspector had informed her that threatening to kill with a loaded weapon was a grave matter that could see her doing several years in prison.

She sobbed as she sat on the lounge floor. Her wrist swollen and blue from Max's bite.

'Laura, now would be a good time to come clean,' the Inspector suggested to her. 'If you co-operate now, it will reduce your sentence considerably.'

'What on earth do you mean?' she sobbed.

'Well, it's clear now that you are responsible for the murder of Abigail McGill.'

She protested her innocence, but the pain from her wrist and the crashing back to reality were taking its toll. Her head swirled around. The lights of the room all rolling around into one ball of light causing her to become nauseous.

Meg had called an ambulance to come and see to her broken wrist. They arrived to find Laura passed out from the pain and the effects of the drink. After some commotion, they managed to get her into the back of the ambulance to take her off to Plymouth Hospital.

Inspector Reynolds instructed Constable Daniels to go in the ambulance with her. 'The moment she's awake you place her under arrest for the murder of Abigail McGill and threatening to kill Lady Carter with a loaded weapon.'

Once the ambulance departed, the Inspector joined Susie and Meg in the Kitchen.

'What will happen from here Inspector?' Meg asked.

'I dare say she will wake up full of regret about the situation.'

'I should hope so. Poor woman needs to seek help for all of her drinking.' Susie said.

'Indeed, she does!' the Inspector agreed.

'Will you be arresting her for the murder of the Mayor then?'

'Yes, I believe we will. It seems she was motivated enough to murder those who she believed had slept with her Dougy.'

Susie explained that Douglas Hamilton had visited her earlier in the night. They had discussed the property deal that he and the old man Ash had been working on. She thought that Laura must have seen him come over and just assumed he was up to no good again. She also mentioned the fact he came back a second time and was quite menacing in his demeanor.

Max who had been in the lounge sniffing everything came into the Kitchen. He sniffed each of them in turn before giving a great big bark of happiness. He found his bed in the corner of the kitchen and curled up as they all laughed at him. The laughter was more of relief that all turned out okay.

'Well, I must depart. My wife will be wondering where I am,' the Inspector said.

Susie and Meg assured him they would be fine with such gallant men in the house as Woolsworth and Max. He bid them good night and headed back home to his cottage in Polmerton.

Meg made them both a hot chocolate with extra marsh mellows, and they sat together in the kitchen enjoying the refreshing taste of the sweet delights.

'Now young Meg, tell me all about your night?'

Meg beamed with delight. In all the excitement of rescuing Susie and Woolsworth, she had to put the thought of her lovely evening out of her mind. Now as she thought back a warm glow filled her face.

'Oh, we had a lovely time. We talked and chatted all night.'

'Oh, that is wonderful dear.' Susie pinched another marshmallow from the bag.

'And you will never guess what?'

'What then?' Susie said with a smile.

'Well he kissed me,' Meg said deliriously with happiness. 'Actually, I kissed him first. I wasn't going to wait around for him to kiss me or I might have been an old maid by then.'

The two of them laughed at the thought. The young Constable still nervous about taking the initiative, though after his performance tonight Susie assured Meg, he was turning into a fine young man.

'So, will we hear wedding bells in the future then?' Susie teased her.

'Ooh, I hope so, but not just yet.' She laughed. 'It was only our first date.'

They laughed some more before heading off to bed. Susie invited Max to sleep at the end of her bed that night. He didn't need to be asked twice and quickly found himself a comfy spot pressed firmly against her leg.

16

The next morning Susie was asked to come to the police station to make a statement. She sat down with the Inspector, and they discussed the turn of events.

Susie went into detail about the visit from Douglas Hamilton and what they discussed. She also explained how he returned shortly after that, and feeling threatened by him.

Step by step, Susie went into detail about how Laura just appeared out of nowhere in the hall with the gun. She concluded she must have followed her husband up to the castle when he returned. She possibly slipped in through the servant's entry at the back while her husband talked with Susie.

Then the tense standoff that led to the breaking of the vase. Upon which Woolsworth awoke and called the Inspector. Right through to the Inspector arriving on the scene, and the final showdown with Max saving the day.

It took some time to get the statement down as the Inspector was not exactly the fastest typist in the world. He pecked away at the keyboard with two fingers as Susie slowly recounted each of the events of the night.

Eventually, after a couple of hours, the statement was complete, and the Inspector printed it out for her to read and sign.

With her statement finished, she visited briefly with Hunter before returning to her car to make her way back home. She had planned to have a quiet afternoon and evening. Perhaps a spot of gardening with Max if the weather cleared. She stopped in at the hardware and garden supplies store to get some fertilizer and some fresh new roses to plant around the rotunda.

The sun had just broken through the clouds as Susie turned the soil in the garden bed. The last two hours were devoted to pulling out the weeds first, then planting the fresh new roses. Max wandered around the yard enjoying the outdoor time.

Susie wiped the sweat from her brow.

Not as fit as I should be she thought to herself. Probably because of all the Cornish treats she had become accustomed to eating. She decided she needed to cut back a bit on the tea parties and add a bit more exercise.

Fortunately, she loved to tend the garden, and it did amount to an adequate level of exercise, so she had been informed.

But the thing she loved the most about the garden was that she spent time without thinking. Her mind became focused on the job at hand, and all of life's troubles seemed to disappear.

As she worked away preoccupied with dishing out the fertilizer in the right quantities, she didn't notice him walking up behind her. Max had drifted off into the woods chasing a rabbit.

He moved swiftly behind her. Coming across the lawn, he didn't make a sound.

As he got closer to Susie, he cast a shadow.

And that's when she first realized he was behind her. His shadow appeared over the garden bed she was working on. Adrenaline flooded her system causing her heart to give an all mighty thump.

Down on all fours and with her back to him she felt extremely vulnerable. She did a quick calculation and remembered Woolsworth had taken the day off and Meg was in town doing a few messages. She was all alone again.

She froze in her tracks.

'Lady Carter?' The voice was unfamiliar, younger with a touch of uncertainty about it. Susie swung around to see who had given her such a fright. Still down on her knees, she looked up.

'Yes, can I help you?'

MURDER AT ASH CASTLE

He was young. Perhaps in his mid-twenties. A good-looking chap who looked like an athlete. He was lean yet muscular with flowing blond hair to his shoulders. He reminded Susie of the surfer boys she saw on a TV show once about Bondi Beach in Australia.

'I wondered if I might have a word?' he said nervously. 'It's a rather delicate matter, and I'm not sure who to go to with it?'

'Yes, of course, young man,' Susie said feeling more relaxed. 'And what is your name?'

Peter Johnson explained to Susie that he was the estate manager for the Hamilton's. The two of them walked inside together to the kitchen to put the kettle on. Susie said she always preferred to chat over a pot of tea as it made the conversation flow. To her delight he readily agreed with her, adding his mother always said the same thing.

'Now Peter, what seems to be troubling you?'

'Well, I am not sure where to start really.' He said nerves overcoming him.

'Give it your best shot,' Susie encouraged him.

For the next few minutes, Peter explained how he had been working for the Hamilton's for the last few years. He lived in the caretaker's cottage at the rear of the estate. From Susie's balcony, she could see the roof of the cottage. He went on about how much he enjoyed the work, looking after the animals that grazed in the fields and taking care of the yards and gardens and the like.

He also shared with Susie how the Hamilton's were extremely busy people. Mr. Hamilton worked long hours and would often travel out of town or up to London on business.

A look of concern came over his face as he started to move to the actual point of the story.

'Well, that all sounds lovely Peter. So, what on earth is troubling you?'

'Oh, is it that obvious that I am troubled?'

'Well yes frankly,' she laughed. 'Perhaps you will feel better when you get it out in the open instead of letting it eat you up inside.'

He thought about it for a moment and decided she was right.

'I'm having an affair with her!' he blurted out making the big announcement.

Susie was shocked for a moment. Who was he referring to she wondered? Several faces came to mind, but none made sense.

123

She tried to maintain her composure and not let the shock register on her face.

'With who dear?'

'Well, with Laura of course.'

'Agghhh,' Susie sighed understanding now why he was so nervous about the matter.

As a formal model, Laura still was one of the most attractive women in Polmerton. It is no wonder that a handsome young fellow like Peter would be attracted to her and her to him. It all made sense.

'You're shocked I guess.'

'Well somewhat, but it's not for me to judge dear.'

'I just had to tell someone. It has been eating me inside with all the recent events.'

Susie thought about it for a moment. Laura had been outraged at her own husband having an affair, to the point where it looks likely she was the culprit in the Mayor's murder, yet the whole time she was doing the same thing.

'Well, how did this all start?'

Peter explained that from the moment he came to work for the Hamilton's, there had been a strong chemistry between them. He had resisted her advances for some months wanting to ensure he kept his job, but eventually, the temptation grew too strong. He was a man after all, he assured Susie.

Susie listened on as Peter explained their various liaisons.

'Well, it seems such a pity that she appears to be the one who did the Mayor in then I'm sorry to say.'

'Oh, she didn't kill the Mayor, she couldn't have.'

There was a certainty about his tone and manner that made Susie believe he was telling the truth. But she had to get to the bottom of why he was so certain.

'Why is that dear?'

'Because she was with me in my bed at the time of the murder.'

'She was?' Susie said startled.

'Yes,' Peter explained, 'After Mr. Hamilton brought her back from the party, and I believe he returned to the party, she came and pounded on my door.'

'I see.'

'I let her in of course. I could tell she was drunk. So, I put her in my bed, and I slept on the couch.'

'She was rather drunk.'

'Indeed, she was. She passed out straight away and slept through to seven thirty the next morning. Snored her head off'

'So, you are saying she couldn't have returned to the party to kill the Mayor then?'

'Not a chance.'

Susie pondered this new breakthrough carefully. He seemed quite a credible young man, but after what she experienced with Laura last night she did believe she was capable of the crime.

'Douglas Hamilton didn't put you up to this did he?'

'I'm sorry, what do you mean?'

'Well I mean he didn't pay you to come and provide Laura with an alibi, did he?'

Peter laughed at the thought. The truth is he wouldn't put it past Mr. Hamilton to do such a thing. But no, not on this occasion. He was probably happy his wife was being locked up.

'Definitely not, no.'

Susie paused for a moment longer. She believed the young man.

'And besides your say so, do you have any proof she was with you?'

Peter thought about it for a moment. He didn't have any proof, just his word. He had hoped his word would have been good enough. His father had always said that if a man isn't as good as his word, then he has nothing left.

'I am afraid I don't have any proof of such, no.'

'I see. Well, you will need to give a full statement to the police, and it will be up to them then whether they will believe you or not I guess.'

'Oh, wait a minute.' He said and whipped out his mobile phone. 'I almost forgot. She was very drunk at the time you know ...'

'Oh, I don't want to see any pictures of the two of you.' Susie interrupted his train of thought.

Peter laughed again. Mostly from the relief of remembering he had the pictures as proof.

'No, nothing like that.'

'Thank goodness.'

'No, she insisted we take some selfies.'

'Selfies?' Susie asked rather bemused. She wasn't sure what a selfie was though she had heard Meg use the term on the odd occasion.

He showed her the pictures. The two of them together, one very drunk looking Laura Hamilton with her mascara having run down the side of her face.

'Yes, but these could have been taken at any time?'

'True, however, every photo you take has a time and date stamp in the file.'

'So, we could find out the date and time you took them then?'

'Yes easily.'

After a brief discussion, Susie hung up the phone. The Inspector was very appreciative of the news of the breakthrough in the case.

He informed her that while this might clear Laura Hamilton of any wrongdoing in the murder of Mayor Abigail McGill, she was still facing charges of holding her and Woolsworth at gunpoint.

The Inspector asked Susie to send the young man down to the station right away. They would record his statement of the events of the night, and request copies of the selfies as evidence.

Susie updated Peter on the conversation with the Inspector once she hung up the phone. She made it clear to Peter that Laura is most likely facing prison time for the intrusion, taking people hostage, and threatening to kill with a loaded weapon.

He looked genuinely sad as he listened, taking it all in.

A short time later he hugged Susie for offering a kind ear. He assured her he felt a lot better now that he had it off his chest. He bid her farewell and departed to go into town to meet with the Inspector.

Susie waved him off and then went back out to the garden where she found her gloves and slipped them back on.

Max had found himself a shady spot under the old oak tree. The sunny day was making him hot, he relaxed and panted, smiling at Susie as she resumed her gardening.

17

Inspector Reynolds was hopping mad when he sat in Susie's lounge room. His cup of tea in one hand and a half-eaten shortbread resting on his knee.

He was busy expressing his frustration with the case to Susie who listened on.

She could certainly understand why he was so frustrated.

Both the prime suspects in the case had proved to have solid alibis, and his prime witness lacked credibility.

She poured another cup of tea while he reviewed the facts in the case. He was starting to take this personally; she thought to herself, as he recounted the murder scene.

'What puzzles me,' he said with a worried look, 'is that the culprit was able to slip out of the poolroom, hide the murder weapon and disappear in the few minutes before Hunter McGill arrived on the scene.

'Yes, good point.'

'How did they leave the poolroom with a fire poker in hand, presumably with blood on it, unnoticed?'

'Again, a very good point.'

Susie had given the same questions some consideration but had not yet arrived at a satisfactory conclusion. The best she had come up with she informed the Inspector, was that the culprit was still in the poolroom when Hunter and Jess Muller had entered. He could have hidden behind the large velvet curtains for a time undetected.

'What and then slipped out when they both ran out of the pool room screaming?'

'It's a possibility.'

'It's not much to go on, but perhaps we should consider it.' He said as he finished off the remainder of the shortbread.

Meg wandered into the lounge and greeted the Inspector. She took a seat next to Susie and poured herself a cup of tea with two sugars. She asked them what they were discussing.

'We were just asking how the killer might have gotten out of the pool room with the murder weapon.' Susie updated her.

'With the murder weapon in hand!' the Inspector emphasised.

Meg gave them a look of surprise. To her it was obvious.

'Wouldn't they have gone through the secret passage behind the bookshelves?' she asked.

The Inspector and Susie exchanged looks. It would explain a lot Susie thought. They could have hit Abigail over the head, knocking her down. Then picked up the fire iron and slipped out through the secret passage behind the bookshelves just as Hunter was coming through the main entrance.

'Yes, you are quite right Meg. Whoever killed the Mayor must have known about the secret passage.' Susie said. She was mentally putting all the pieces together on what had taken place.

'Where does this secret passage lead to then?' the Inspector asked.

'Back to the servant's quarters. I used to play in there as a child.'

'So, the big question then is who knows there is a secret passage from the pool room?'

'Oh well, that is an easy question to answer.' Meg said with confidence.

'Go on?'

'Well, it hasn't been used for decades. I would say the only people who really knew about it would have been Charles Ash, Woolsworth and me.'

As Meg said the words aloud, it dawned on her the implications of what she was saying. With Ash already dead that left just her and Woolsworth. And she knew that it wasn't her. That just left Woolsworth.

Catching her train of thought both Susie and the Inspector arrived at the same conclusion at the same time. All three of them sat there in a state of shock.

'No, it couldn't have been.' Meg decided flatly refusing to believe it was possible. She had known Woolsworth her entire life. He practically raised her. Aside from his grumpy disposition, there was nothing in his character that would have suggested murder.

Susie agreed it seemed unlikely but didn't rule the idea out completely.

'Well it would be awfully cliché for the butler to have done it,' the Inspector said with a failed attempt at humor. 'But we cannot rule out any possibility now.'

'So, assuming it was Woolsworth then he would have known the passage was there to make good his escape. But where would he have put the murder weapon?' Susie asked.

'Well, he either left it in the passage. He could return to collect it later when the commotion had settled down.'

'Or he hid it in his quarters.' The inspector finished.

Meg agreed to show them the secret passage. All three of them and Max filed into the pool room. Max was happy. He could sense the excitement in the air as he weaved his way in between the legs of the humans.

The large bookcase on the far wall appeared to be the one. Meg walked up to it and started pulling at the books on the shelves. Then she found the one she was looking for. It was a red leather-bound copy of the King James Version of the Bible. She pulled it towards her from the top activating a hidden switch.

In turn, the switch turned on the mechanism which enables the bookshelves to be easily moved a meter to the right-hand side.

And there it was before them, a small dark musky smelling passage. It provided adequate height for those under five feet tall Susie thought. The paneled walls lined with candlestick holders.

'In the old days, this passage would have been used by the serving staff to bring refreshments to those in the pool room.' Meg informed them as she stepped into the dark.

'Or, for those wanting to make good their escape,' the Inspector snarled.

Max darted on ahead of Meg eager to get to the other side. And to see what there was to sniff. And maybe even to eat if he was lucky.

Susie and the Inspector followed Meg taking a step of faith into the unknown. It was pitch black ahead, and they all hoped they wouldn't be tripping over any dead bodies today.

The only remaining light from the pool table disappeared over their shoulders as they rounded the corner.

Then it went pitch black.

Susie couldn't see her hand in front of her face.

She wondered if this is what it would have been like for all those coal miners in the south Yorkshire mines. Her own grandfather had been a miner since his childhood days.

Max started barking frantically.

His paws scratching at a wooden door.

'What is it, Max?' Susie asked concerned about his frantic manner.

'The door,' Meg sighed. 'It's locked.'

'What door?' the Inspector inquired.

Meg tried to force the door that opened into the servant's quarters, open. It wouldn't budge. She pushed both her shoulder and knee against it, but the door was not moving.

'Let me try then,' the Inspector said, thinking Meg too petite to have much impact on the old door hinges.

He stepped back and then threw himself hard against the door. The door didn't budge, but he did, bouncing right off it and crashing back into Meg and Susie.

'Seems to be locked from the other side,' he exclaimed eagerly to excuse his failure.

'Locked?' Meg said with a sinking feeling. 'That's not good.'

Meg ran back to the pool room but as she suspected the bookcase had returned to its position concealing the entrance to the passage. There was no way to open it from the inside.

'Well?' Susie asked feeling anxious.

'No good it's locked from the outside' Meg said.

Susie felt a twinge of panic starting in her gut. She wasn't afraid of many things in life except being stuck in a small dark space.

She had suffered from claustrophobia most of her life. Mostly it was kept under control. But this situation had the makings of a major panic attack if they didn't get out of this place real soon.

Inspector Reynolds heard something on the other side of the door. It sounded like talking. They decided it could only be one person.

Woolsworth.

They cried out for help, but it was of little use. Woolsworth had started losing his hearing twenty years ago. There was not much hope that he would hear them through the thick walls.

Meg pressed her ear up to the door to the servant's quarters to listen. She could hear Woolsworth. It sounded like he was shouting at the top of his voice.

She couldn't quite make out what he was saying, but it sounded a little along the lines of 'I have you all trapped now. You are all going to die in there.'

Meg screamed in despair and banged on the door. Max barked wildly, wanting to be let out. The one person who could save them was also plotting to kill them, she thought.

Leaning against the wall, Susie was starting to feel nauseous. Sweat gathered on her forehead and the back of her neck. Her head started spinning. She had to sit down before she fainted. Her knees buckled, and she slid down the wall and plonked on the floor.

Max came rushing over. He could sense she was not feeling great. Somehow, he just knew that he had to get help for her.

After several more attempts to get Woolsworth's attention, or to knock the door down, both Meg and the Inspector joined Susie on the floor.

Unable to see in the dark, and with little possibility of freeing themselves, they felt it best to conserve their energy for now. The temperature in the passageway had climbed significantly. The level of oxygen was starting to drop.

Inspector Reynolds sat slumped forward. Exhaustion had caught up with him. The small passage that entombed them had become stifling hot. His shirt was soaked in sweat. His breathing more labored.

He watched as both Susie and Meg fell asleep.

Attempting to glance at his watch he assumed they had been trapped for a good two hours or more. But he couldn't be sure as he was unable to see the time.

His mind drifted back to the conversation they were having just before Susie fell asleep. Talk had been on the fact that only Woolsworth and Meg had known about this secret passage and how to open it. With Meg trapped inside with them both, the Inspector and Susie agreed that the spotlight of guilt was now firmly focused on Woolsworth.

Susie was unsure about his motives.

But she was clear on one thing that they had been lured into a trap. They decided that they were best to wait until they heard a noise in the house before they tried to raise the alarm again.

The Inspector was starting to fall asleep himself when he realized he hadn't seen Max in some time. He leaned over Susie to see if he was sitting on the other side of her, but he was not. Strange he thought to himself.

His eyes heavy he started to drift off.

In his mind, he was floating in space, a vast dark nothingness. He was enjoying the feeling of weightlessness, of just drifting in the dark.

Then a small slither of light appeared. Strange he thought that a sliver of light should appear out of nowhere.

The sliver of light was followed by voices. Muffled at first but becoming clearer. Then a bark.

He snapped himself awake. That was no dream he realized as he quickly shook both Meg and Susie awake. The sliver of light grew wider as the old door to the servant's quarters was being forced open from the outside.

Familiar voices helped all three of them feel better.

Finally, the door gave up its hold and opened with a creak. It reminded Susie of an old black and white horror film.

Max leaped in through the now open doorway to check they were all okay. He barked and licked each of them, in turn, delighted they were okay. His tail stirring the dust and cobwebs as he thumped it from side to side.

'Everyone okay?' Douglas Hamilton asked helping the Inspector out into the light of day.

'I believe so.' The Inspector said checking in with Meg and Susie.

'How did you find us here?' Susie asked.

'It was the wretched beast Ma'am' Woolsworth said. He explained how Max had appeared out of nowhere in his room barking and causing a commotion. Max had led him back to the door to the passage where he realized they must be trapped.

Unable to budge the door open himself Woolsworth had called Douglas Hamilton to come and assist. Douglas had come straight away and managed to wedge the door open with a crowbar.

'Oh, Max you saved the day.' Meg said hugging him. 'But how did you get out of the passage?'

Douglas Hamilton was examining a small heating vent on the side of the wall near the passage. The grill to the air vent had been knocked out and was on the floor.

'Looks like he found a way out through the heating vents here,' Hamilton explained.

On seeing Hamilton looking into the vent, Max rushed over. He poked his muzzle into the vent and started barking frantically. He pawed at the edge of the vent. His barking was quite insistent like he was trying to tell them all something.

'What is it, Max?'

The Inspector looked inside. He asked Woolsworth for a flashlight to take a closer look.

'How on earth did you get through there then Max?' he asked.

Max gave a bark which caused them all to laugh.

'The beast was covered in cobwebs and muck.' Woolsworth said less than impressed. 'I'm not sure how he found the vent. I've been here my entire life and never noticed its existence.'

The Inspector looked in the vent and noticed something sticking out at the bend. He reached in and took hold of something cold and metallic. Carefully he worked it around the bend and eased it out into the light of day.

They all gathered around to see what it was. In his hand, he held out the fire iron from the lounge. The jagged end appeared to have blood stains on it and possibly fragments of hair. He placed it on a small side table and asked Woolsworth for a plastic bag.

'Looks like the culprit had enough knowledge to know there was a heating vent here to hide the murder weapon in then,' the Inspector said.

'Best we get that off too forensics I suspect.' Susie said.

'Could it tell us who the killer is?' Meg asked.

The Inspector explained that they would need to get it dusted for fingerprints. If they could get one clear print, then they could use it to trace the killer. Especially if the killer already had their prints recorded in the police database.

Either way, it was the first real clue they had in the case that might prove to be evidence in tracking down the killer.

18

Susie sat bolt upright in bed.

She knew who it was. The answer had come to her like a bolt of lightning. It was so obvious she had mostly overlooked it. But it could only be him.

She was quickly up, showered and dressed for breakfast. There was a spring in her step as she knew that she was close to resolving the murder. Once this mess was all cleared up, she would be free to focus on more exciting things like the cooking school.

After breakfast, she telephoned the Inspector.

'I know who it was,' she squealed down the phone.

'Oh right, who's that then?'

'I won't say over the phone. But can you come at eleven?'

They discussed the details. She explained how she was going to organize a tea party and invite the culprit to join her. She would then bring in the Inspector and reveal all, leaving him to make the arrest.

'Right-oh then,' he agreed. 'We might even have a report back from forensics by then.'

'Oh, and can you bring all the witness statements from the night?'

She hung up the phone. She felt nervous about making the call to him though he had always been very pleasant to her. But she must do it, she told herself for the sake of everyone concerned.

Searching through her purse, she found his card. He had given it to her at the party, and she stored it away for safekeeping. Now holding it in her hand, a flood of adrenaline came over her.

She picked up the phone and dialed the number. The phone rang twice before he answered. His voice, a little harsh like he had been interrupted.

'Oh hello, its Susie Carter here, how are you?'

He cheered up at hearing her voice. 'Oh, I'm very well thank you, Lady Carter, and you?'

They made small talk for a moment about the weather and the like which Susie had decided was the custom for local folks.

'So, I am having a tea party at eleven with a few guests and wondering if you would join us?'

He heartily agreed and said he would see her then.

She hung up the phone.

Next, she needed to invite several other guests. First on the list was Hunter. She explained her plan to him. Most definitely he assured her and offered to bring some treats.

A few more phone calls and all was in order.

The tea party was well underway in the lounge room by eleven. It had been raining heavily outside, so the rotunda was not an option. The open fire crackled creating a cozy atmosphere.

Heath Henshaw stood with his back to the fire warming his hands. He was chatting with Councilor Bradshaw and Douglas Hamilton. Seated on the couch engrossed in conversation was Meg with Jess Fuller, her husband and Constable Daniels.

Woolsworth was busy ensuring fresh pots of tea were available for everyone. Hunter proudly offering around his scones which were greeted with much delight. Max was happy as he was getting pats from all directions.

The Inspector was engrossed in conversation with the Aunties. They were discussing a case from a few years ago where a local identity was caught trying to embezzle funds out of the law firm's trust account. The Aunties, of course, knew all the details of the case which they had gathered on the grapevine.

Susie surveyed the scene before her. In this room, she was sure the murderer of Mayor Abigail McGill was partaking in her hospitality. Now it was time to hand them over to the Inspector, so she could put this whole mess behind her.

She picked up a glass and a small teaspoon and gently tapped the side to get their attention. Slowly conversation turned to murmurs and whispers.

'I just wanted to thank you all for coming, especially at such short notice.' She said to them. They all gave her a cheer of thanks back loving a good gathering and a gossip.

'I suppose you are all wondering why I have asked you here. So, I just need a moment of your time.' Susie said searching for the right words. 'You see, I wanted to get to the bottom of this whole mess with the Mayor.'

'Oh yes, how is the investigation progressing?' asked Henshaw leaning on the mantle.

'Well, that's what we are here for now, to resolve the investigation,' she said nodding to the Inspector. 'It seems we have narrowed down the killer to one of us in this room.'

A gasp filled the air as they each considered the possibility that they were chatting with a murderer.

'So, who on earth was it?' Mildred asked delirious with excitement.

'Well at first everyone thought it was Hunter' Susie said nodding to Hunter. 'Young Jess here was clearly disturbed by what she saw and gave a good account of how she saw a blood-soaked Hunter at the scene of the crime.'

Jess's husband squeezed her hand in support.

'But as it turned out, Hunter was not present at the time of the murder. I had considered the possibility that as you Jess were first on the scene besides Hunter, that you would have had time to do it, but it seemed unlikely as you had no real motive that I was aware of.'

Hunter breathed a sigh of relief and dove in for another scone.

'So, then I suspected that Mr. Henshaw might have had a motive as the Mayor had blocked his plans to develop apartments in town.'

'Yes, but as I pointed out, that was just one development of many.' Henshaw said smugly.

'Quite right Mr. Henshaw.' Susie agreed. 'Douglas Hamilton,' she said, staring straight at him. 'It seems you had a motive larger than anyone here given your affair with the Mayor.'

Shocked that he felt the finger pointed at him, he protested his innocence.

'Yes well, you did give me quite a fright the other night you know. However, I don't think you did it, more likely your outraged wife!'

'Oh yes, Laura was hopping mad at Abigail.' Mildred said.

'And put on a turn at the party!' Mabel agreed.

'Clearly, she is guilty of threatening to kill with a deadly weapon,' the Inspector added.

'Yes, very much so, and at the time I thought she had the capability and the motive to commit murder. But then a rather strange turn of events occurred the other day when I had a visitor.'

'From who?' Douglas Hamilton demanded to know.

'From your yard boy, he has proof that he was in bed with your wife at the time of the murder Mr. Hamilton.' Susie said thinking it was best he heard the truth.

Douglas Hamilton's face went red, and he slammed his fist on the mantle in a rage. Susie ignored him.

'As the investigation went on, it became clear that whoever the culprit was, had to have known about the secret passageway that led from the pool room to the servant's quarters. It seems that after killing the Mayor, they slipped through the secret passage with the murder weapon to avoid being noticed. Shortly after, Hunter walked in on the scene.'

'Well that narrows it down then.' Henshaw said staring straight at Woolsworth.

'Secret passage?' Mabel asked intrigued.

'It does narrow it down indeed. Not even I knew about the passageway. As Meg informed me the only two people she was aware of who knew are herself and Woolsworth. As Meg was with me the whole night, it couldn't have been her.'

Everyone gasped.

'The butler did it?' Mildred asked seeking confirmation.

Woolsworth sat there silent. His face was expressionless.

'How awfully cliché of you old chap.' Henshaw joked.

'I would never have killed someone who was close to Charles!' Woolsworth objected.

'Quite right Woolsworth. You may have had knowledge of the passageway, but you lacked in motive, and I am certain that while your disposition is not always agreeable, you are not capable of murder.'

'So, where does that leave us all then?' Hunter asked wanting to get to the bottom of it.

'Well, it seems that the most likely scenario is that whoever did it had a strong motivation, and knew the secret passage was there, but also wanted to frame Woolsworth here by making it look like he did it.'

The Inspector was taking notes as Susie talked. He now glanced around the room. Even he was unclear who it could have been. Puzzled looks came across all the faces presents.

'And I have a hunch that the guilty party was not one of those who Constable Daniels here had an opportunity to take a statement from.'

'How is that possible?' Mildred asked with disbelief.

'Because whoever did it slipped out the servants' door and escaped into the night while the commotion was going on inside.'

Everyone started talking at once, trying to work out who the guilty party was.

'Okay, everyone. I am getting to the point. I have had Constable Daniels here go through all the statements taken on the night to see whose statement is missing. So, what have you found?' she asked turning to Daniels.

Daniels cleared his throat. 'Well yes, there is one person here who was not around to give a statement.'

'And that person is our Murderer!' Susie finished off.

'Isn't that right Councilor Bradshaw?' she asked staring straight at him.

Mildred and Mabel both nearly died with shock. They had known Bradshaw for years and would never have suspected he had a violent streak in his body.

Bradshaw remained calm. He simply returned Susie's gaze waiting for her to present her case.

At sixty-nine years of age, his face was aged beyond his years. His body still fit and strong though and was certainly strong enough to hit a woman over the head with a fire iron.

He had been on the local council for twenty-five years or more, and the local historian since a teenager. Most who knew him thought he was a fine upstanding member of the community.

'Well, what do you say to the accusation?' Henshaw asked impatiently.

'At this stage, I have nothing to say until I hear what evidence is against me?' Bradshaw said raising his voice as he spoke. 'It seems to me that this whole thing has been a bit of a witch hunt. And as the others didn't turn out to be witches, then it's my turn to be accused.'

'The evidence appears obvious.' Susie said as everyone leaned forward waiting to hear it with bated breath.

'Go on then,' he urged her.

'You planned to meet with the Mayor in the pool room where you knew there wouldn't be anyone from the party. Before that, you had sneaked around to the servant's quarters. Everyone was busy at the party. So you made sure the exit door to the secret passage was open.

Bradshaw said nothing as he listened.

'You then entered the lounge also via the servant's entry and grabbed the fire poker before returning to the pool room where the Mayor was waiting for you. She was quite drunk, and a brief argument took place.'

Bradshaw smiled as she continued. She had much of the story wrong.

'When she went to walk out of the pool room, you hit her in the head, a single fatal blow causing her to fall forward, her head then hitting both the pool table and the slate floor as she fell.'

Inspector Reynolds phone buzzed in his pocket. He read the text message as he listened to Susie. He had to read the message twice before he cleared his throat.

'Lady Carter we have had a confirmation from Emma in Forensics that she has found prints on the murder weapon.'

He chose his words carefully as much for dramatic effect as anything else.

'Excellent news.' Susie said a smile filling her face. 'There is no hiding for the murderer now.'

Bradshaw's energy changed. He went from defiant to defeat in seconds.

'After striking the fatal blow, you exited the pool room via the secret passage behind the bookshelves, the same passage that only a handful of people knew even existed.'

'But how did Bradshaw know about it then?' Mabel interjected wanting to get all the facts right.

'Simple. Bradshaw is the town historian with a specialty in Castles in the Cornwall area. He had befriended Charles many years ago and was one of the few people who ever got the full tour of the castle. Isn't that right?'

He nodded in agreement.

Susie went on to explain how after hitting her in the head he went out through the secret passage returning the bookshelves to their natural place. He hid the fire poker in the heating vent and then left the building through the rear door of the servant's quarters. Because he wasn't present when the body was found, he was never considered as a witness until now.

'She's lying! I didn't do it.' Bradshaw claimed.

'But what was your motive old boy?' Henshaw was dying to find out.

'I think I have worked that out too.' Susie said, though inside she wasn't entirely sure she had it correct. 'Councilor Bradshaw here was aware that Mayor Abigail McGill was the only child of Charles Ash III.' Susie said dropping a bombshell that only Woolsworth was not shocked by.

'No?' cried out Mabel.

'Well you think you know someone.' Mildred added.

'But, wait a minute,' Henshaw interrupted. 'If she was his child then by rights she should have inherited the castle?'

Everyone agreed with Henshaw. Surely the castle and estate should have gone to Abigail if such a thing were true.

Woolsworth was becoming distressed that family secrets were spilling. He thought he best put a stop to things before they got out of hand.

'Bastard child!' Woolsworth cried out over the noise of the room.

'I beg your pardon Woolsworth?' Mable said horrified.

'She was the bastard child of Mr. Ash. He never accepted her as his own despite her pleas. All she ever wanted really was a father, but he didn't have it in his heart to acknowledge what he had done.'

Woolworth's heart sped up. His palms had turned sweaty. He just prayed that this was as deep as anyone dared go into the affairs of Charles Ash III.

'She tried everything to get the old man Ash to leave her the estate.' Bradshaw said to the disbelief of all gathered. 'And she nearly succeeded too. At one stage he did draw up a will with her as the sole beneficiary.'

'Goodness me no,' Mabel said stunned at the news.

'And what happened?' Mildred needs to know.

'He changed his mind and hid the will somewhere in the castle, somewhere safe that only he knew. Then he drew up a new and most recent will that superseded it.' Woolsworth explained.

'But Abigail was convinced the will, leaving it all to her, was still hidden somewhere. That's why she agreed to meeting me in the pool room that night.' Bradshaw said.

'Yes, you were the one person who could locate it for her.'

'You are right Lady Carter, but of course, I refused to do so.'

'And why is that?'

'Because I didn't want her to get her hands-on Ash Castle and turn it into a hotel. That's what they were planning.' Bradshaw nodded towards Douglas Hamilton who had remained silent throughout.

'Yes, that explains why Mr. Hamilton was trying to blackmail Charles. He was threatening to tell the world about Charles Ash's real secrets. He and Abigail plotted to bankrupt Charles first and then step in to help. Along the way convincing him to leave the castle to her.'

A look of shame came across the face and body of Douglas Hamilton.

'So, Councilor Bradshaw, I put it to you that you had both the motive and the means to carry out the murder of Mayor Abigail McGill.'

The Inspector stood up. He carefully folded his notebook up and slipped it into his pants pocket.

'Well, what do you say?' Henshaw urged him.

'I didn't kill her no.' Bradshaw responded. Fear was now gripping him as he considered the consequences of his actions. 'Well, I mean, I didn't intend to kill her. It was her that came at me with the fire poker. She was in a rage with me for not helping her find the old will. I told her I never would. She swung the fire iron at me several times. One of the blows hit me on the shoulder.'

He pulled his jumper down revealing the bruise.

'I was frightened for my life. I'm not a violent man you know,' his face was now red. Tears welling up in his eyes as he recalled the events of the night.

'When she swung it at me a third time, I grabbed it off her. Had to wrestle it out of her hands.' Bradshaw said with a shaky, nervous voice. 'She came at me again, so I swung at her to stop her. I didn't mean to kill her though.'

Everyone was shocked. Silence filled the room.

You could hear a clock tick as they all mentally went through the events of the night.

Bradshaw sobbed. He was glad it was all out in the open.

'I only ever wanted to protect Ash Castle.'

Inspector Bradshaw walked over to the Councilor and informed him he was under arrest for the murder of the Mayor and he would be taken back to the station for questioning.

As they were about to depart the lounge room, the Inspector turned back to them and said 'Oh and Mr. Hamilton, I will be coming to discuss the matter of blackmailing old man Ash with you. So, don't leave town.'

Douglas Hamilton just sighed with despair. He wondered why he ever let that Abigail McGill use and manipulate him the way she had. He walked over to the drinks cabinet and poured himself a seven-year-old scotch and downed it in one mouthful.

'Well done, Lady Carter. It seems you are quite the amateur sleuth and have cracked the case wide open.' Henshaw said, and they all gave a half-hearted cheer.

'Yes, well I am just glad it's all over now.'

Susie went to pour herself a stiff drink when Woolsworth stood up and announced he had something to say, something shocking.

They all were surprised as Woolsworth rarely spoke to any of them.

'What's that then?' Susie asked filling her glass to the top with scotch.

'He killed him!' Woolsworth blurted out.

'Who killed whom dear?' Mildred asked somewhat confused.

'He killed him!' Woolsworth said now pointing towards Hamilton. 'He killed my beloved Charles.' Woolsworth broke down in tears as he remembered the events of the night Charles Ash passed away.

Douglas Hamilton was taken aback by these fresh allegations, but not surprised. He knew the day would come when Woolsworth would accuse him of it.

'Good heavens Woolsworth. Do you know what you are saying man?' Henshaw was disturbed by the claim.

'He killed Charles. Abigail made him do it. She told him she had the will with the estate in her name, and they needed to remove Charles before it was too late.'

Hamilton had stood up and taken several steps around the back of the couch. 'What rubbish!' he said.

With that, he sprinted towards the door.

Max, sensing the moment, knew he had to act fast. He had been rather comfortable dozing off in front of the fire. But now he knew he needed to make a move.

As Douglas Hamilton bolted for the half-closed door, Max leaped over the coffee table and grabbed his ankle wrestling him to the ground. Constable Daniels, a bit slow to react, jumped up to assist Max.

Hamilton cried out in pain as the lounge room door swung open.

The Inspector stood in the doorway. 'Going somewhere?' he asked Hamilton who was rolling on the floor trying to free Max of his leg.

'Constable Daniels, I believe you will want to bring Mr. Hamilton here, down to the station with us.'

19

Three weeks later and the big day had finally arrived. The first official class of the Cornish Cooking School. A lot had passed since the now infamous tea party, allowing Susie, Meg and Hunter to focus on the task of getting the cooking school launched.

Now with the sun out, the first of the students had arrived for the day-long class. Susie and Meg greeted each of the twelve students as they arrived and showed them into the grand ballroom.

The grand ballroom had been transformed into a cooking school of epic proportions. Rows of tables that held the freshest local ingredients. Each place had its own utensils and gas-powered cooker, a set of knives, chopping board and pots, and pans for each student.

Hunter had arrived early to get everything set up. A trip to the markets at the break of dawn to ensure he had the finest of ingredients that Cornwall had to offer before making his way to Ash Castle.

And now all was set as the students excitedly arrived and took their places.

Many locals were eager to learn how to cook in the traditional Cornish way, like their grandparents had.

More than one of them commented that it was so wonderful the school had started to teach people how to cook the local fair.

Susie and Hunter were delighted with the feedback.

'Perhaps we are onto a winner,' she said to Max as she watched each of the students find their place in the grand ballroom.

Max smiled and nuzzled her leg.

Meg kept herself busy taking photos for the new website and Facebook page. Susie marveled at her and how great she had been helping to pull everything together, despite the dramas that followed the opening night party.

'Well, it all seems in order, Ma'am.' Woolsworth said sounding pleased. 'And it's a credit to you breathing some new life in the old castle.'

For the first time since she arrived, Woolsworth smiled at her.

'Thank you Woolsworth. Very kind of you.'

With all the students at their tables, Hunter signaled Susie to come over and make some opening remarks. She thanked everyone for coming and being among the first ever students of what she hoped would become a well-known feature of the town of Polmerton and of Cornwall itself.

She turned it over to Hunter who was in his element.

He gave them all a hearty welcome, to which they all cheered.

'Right, today we are going to make some local delights. Starting off with Stargazy Pie.'

'Oh, smashing, my favorite that my Nana used to make,' one of the students said excitedly.

'Good-oh' Hunter smiled. 'Then we will follow along with the traditional Cornish pasty with turps, tates and mate. That's turnips, potatoes and mince if you are wondering.'

Another hearty round of cheer and excitement.

'And of course, we will follow this with Hevva Cake and Whortleberry Pie.'

'With lashings of blackberry jam and clotted cream I hope?'

Again, roars of laughter and good cheer all around.

Susie watched on as Hunter led them on a journey through the ingredients and utensils. He showed them good knife skills and how to follow a recipe.

Somehow, she had a feeling that everything was going to be all right. She knew now that she had found her place in the world, and that she and Max would be long-time residents of Ash Castle.

The morning passed without a hitch. By midday, everyone had their Stargazy Pie and Cornish Pasties ready to come out of the ovens.

A large dining table had been set up for everyone to sample what they had just cooked. Meg and Susie pitched in to help serve, while Woolsworth fetched pots of tea.

Susie invited Woolsworth and Meg to join them at the table. 'Are you quite sure Ma'am?' he questioned.

'Indeed Woolsworth. You are as much a part of this as the rest of us.'

He smiled again for the second time. Meg smiled back at him making him realize he was showing too much emotion. He quickly wiped the smile from his face even though he was delighted with the way things had turned out.

When lunch was over, Susie decided it was time to call Margery and give her an update. It had been some time since they had spoken, and Susie felt the need to have a jolly good chin wag with her. She left the class as they made deserts and vowed she would be back for afternoon tea.

'Oh, hello dear, it's so good to hear your voice.' Margery said with relief.

'Oh yes. I am sorry it's taken me so long to call.'

They chatted on for some time.

Susie filled Margery in on all the events of the last few weeks. She explained the night of the party with everything that went wrong, the Mayor having arguments with everyone, Laura Hamilton's attack on her during the speech. Not a detail was left out about the murder and the aftermath.

'Oh, good lord, what a time you have had.' Margery shrieked not able to take it all in. 'How did you catch the killer?'

'Well at first they had it all wrong. It seemed the local Inspector had it in for Hunter McGill and falsely accused him.'

'So, what did you do?'

'Well I stepped in and conducted my own investigations.'

'Quite right dear, you have always had a nose for solving puzzles and things.'

They laughed as Susie explained how they eventually established an alibi for Hunter proving he could not have done it.

Susie recalled the events the night Douglas Hamilton had visited her and then came back again frightening the life out of her. Margery was all ears as she listened in on the moment by moment account of Laura Hamilton pointing a gun at her.

'Oh no, that's not on now, is it?' Margery said sympathetically.

'Not at all. It frightened the life out of me. But then the Inspector burst into the lounge through a servant's entry to save the day. It got me thinking about how the culprit might have escaped the pool room undetected.'

Susie went on to share how they all became trapped in the secret passage in the search for clues, and how Max eventually was the one who found the murder weapon hidden there.

And finally, she got to the part about the tea party and how she finally called out the murderer as Councilor Bradshaw.

'But how on earth did you know it was him?'

'Well, when the Inspector rescued me from Laura Hamilton and the gun episode, I concluded that the killer must have escaped through a secret passage. Therefore, the killer had to have known the castle inside out.'

'Oh yes, I see.'

'And Bradshaw was one of the few who knew about such passageways.'

'But how come dear? How did he know?'

'Turns out he is the town historian with a special interest in local historic castles. When I visited his office one time, he had detailed plans of local castles all over his office wall.'

'Oh well, he knew how to escape the scene of the crime then.'

'Yes, and as it turns out, he had befriended Uncle Charles who had regularly given him detailed tours few others were privy to.'

They chatted for a bit longer about Bradshaw's motives and how the Mayor and the Hamilton's had tried to blackmail Charles to bankrupt him. The grand plan being to turn the castle into apartments for rich Londoners to use as weekenders.

Susie updated Margery about how well the first cooking class was going and what a great job Hunter is doing teaching them all.

'Oh, this Hunter McGill sounds interesting dear?'

Susie blushed. She knew what Margery was inferring.

'Well, we shall see.'

'Do keep me updated on progress then.' Margery laughed.

Her laughter always made Susie happier about everything in life. She did miss her friend so much, but she reasoned that things in life change. Now was the time to tell her she decided.

'There is one other thing Margery'

'What's that dear?'

'Well now that all the drama of the Mayors passing is old news I have found myself becoming very attached to the castle and the town.'

'I see' Margery was all ears though she knew what was coming.

'Yes well, I have decided it might be time for me to sell my cottage and make the move permanent.'

There was a brief pause on the other end of the phone. It seemed like an eternity. She hoped that Margery wouldn't be too upset.

'That's a wonderful idea dear.' Margery said to the relief of Susie. 'You could use the funds to pay down the debts of Ash Castle, do some needed repairs and set things up for success with the cooking school.'

'Oh yes, that's exactly what I was thinking.'

They chatted on excitedly for the next few minutes and promised they would keep in regular contact. They also agreed that Margery would have to come and visit at least several times a year. Relieved that Margery had taken the news so well, she headed back to the class. Eager to sample some Hevva Cake she hoped she wasn't too late for afternoon tea.

20

The last of the student's cars disappeared down the driveway. Susie waved them off and then heaved a sigh of relief. It had been such a wonderful day. The build-up to it though had frankly tired her out. She vowed to take a few days of this week.

Back in the lounge room, she joined Hunter, Meg, Woolsworth and Max.

Meg had a bottle of champagne she had chilled the day before.

The pop of the cork led to a cheer all around. Champagne flowed as they celebrated the success of the first class of the Cornish Cooking School.

Feedback from the students had been wonderful with lots of great testimonials.

Hunter was positively beaming. He proclaimed that this was what he was meant to be doing with his talents and skills, not just working in the bakery. Of course, he loved the bakery, he made the point. Just that he had bigger fish to fry.

Talk turned to the next class in a few weeks' time.

'Oh, and good news to hand,' Hunter announced. He had almost forgotten to share this news with everything that had taken place today. 'Patty Malone had just called to ask about us doing a two-day cooking class as part of the coming Pirates and Wenches Convention.'

'Fabulous news,' Meg said.

'And what on earth is the Pirates and Wenches Convention?' Susie asked somewhat uncertain. She recalled Patty mentioning it but she was unsure of the details.

Meg and Hunter took turns explaining that the Pirates and Wenches Convention was the biggest tourism event in Polmerton each year, possibly the whole of Cornwall. It was a convention for lovers of all things pirates and the like.

'Patty is one of the organizers of the convention. She wants us to be part of it this year.' Hunter explained.

'Patty? Now where did I meet her?'

Meg reminded her she had. 'She owns the Smugglers Inn.'

'Oh yes of course.' Susie laughed. The champagne was making her nice and relaxed.

'Oh, and one other thing,' Hunter said sheepishly.

'Yes?' Susie inquired with some trepidation.

'Well, it seems that she was short an actress for the annual performance of the musical Castaways.'

'Is that right?' Susie was now rather concerned.

'Yes, well she was in a spot of bother with it all. So, I ...'

'No! Never?' Meg proclaimed her hand to her mouth.

'Oh yes I did.' Hunter said to her and roared with laughter. Meg and Woolsworth joined in, and Max thought he should join in with a few barks.

'Come on you lot. What's so funny then?'

'Right yes, as I was saying, she was short an actress for the Castaways Musical. They perform it every year you know.'

Susie was growing impatient. 'Yes, yes get on with it.'

'Well, she asked if you would mind stepping in.' Hunter informed her. 'I said, of course, you would love to be in it.'

Everyone roared with laughter except Susie. She managed a smile, but she was unsure about starting an acting career at her age.

'Did you indeed?'

'It's just a small role.'

Again, more laughter around the lounge room.

'So, is it a speaking part then?' Meg asked.

'I believe it is yes. But there are only a few lines to learn as I understand.'

Susie rolled her eyes in jest. In her wildest dreams did she ever think she would wind up acting in a musical as part of the Pirates and Wenches Convention, but then she never imagined she would own a castle or run a cooking school in Cornwall either.

'And may I inquire as to what part I will be playing then?'

'Oh right, so you will do it then?' Hunter asked joyfully.

'I imagine I have no choice now that you have volunteered me.'

Woolsworth cleared his throat. His mood a lot lighter lately.

'Ma'am, I do believe your part will be that of a wench if you don't mind me saying,' he informed her.

'That's what I was afraid of.' Susie laughed.

'Might have been a bit difficult to cast you as a Pirate' Meg said causing more laughter and good cheer all around.

The bottle of champagne was soon emptied. Everyone was in great spirits when Susie asked, 'So Mr. McGill, I assume you will be one of the pirates then?'

'Indeed, I am yes.'

'I see.' She smiled at him. Her cheeks flushed red.

She thought about it for a moment and decided it might, in fact, be a bit of fun. It would be a great way to meet more of the locals and do all she could to help with the upcoming convention.

'Here's to Pirates and Wenches then.' She said raising her glass and giving Hunter a quick wink.

A cheer went up as they drained their glasses looking forward to the days ahead.

---- THE END -----

ABOUT THE AUTHOR

Jessica Moore is the pen name of an Australian Mystery & Thriller author. After visiting Cornwall in 2010 she fell in love with the charms of the quaint seaside villages and gorgeous countryside. Growing up as a child she was fascinated with castles and pirates. Today Jessica is busy writing more books in the Susie Carter Mystery series.

Printed in Poland
by Amazon Fulfillment
Poland Sp. z o.o., Wrocław

90506002R00096